ZONING

BY
SPENCER KANSA

Published by Beatdom Books

View the author's website:
www.spencerkansa.com

View the publisher's website:
www.books.beatdom.com

Printed in the United Kingdom
First Printing: July 2011
ISBN 978-0-9569525-0-9

CONTENTS

AUTHOR'S ACKNOWLEDGEMENTS
To Poet Dave, whose encouragement, patience and
secretarial skills oversaw this novel during its very earliest
conception.

To Martina Punt and Andy C, who both kindly let me into
their homes to use their PCs so I could work on sections of
this novel. Your hospitality meant everything during those
times.

To Dan Lish, AKA Duce, for creating such a stunningly
beautiful book cover. You can check out more of Dan's
amazing artwork at: www.danlish.com

To my good pal Bari Glew, for the technical assistance he
brought to bear manipulating the front cover image, and for
all the great work he does on my website.

And lastly to my fellow author and pal, Stephen Sennitt, for
kindly proofreading the text.
Boat drinks, SK.

DEDICATION

This book is dedicated to Barbara Snow Phillips, for her aid and assistance above and beyond the call of duty throughout my life. You are appreciated.

"The secret of life is breath." Anais Nin on LSD.

"Everything one does in life, even love, occurs in an express train racing toward death. To smoke opium is to get out of the train while it is still moving. It is to concern oneself with something other than life or death." Jean Cocteau.

"Evil swirls and rushes around your feet, while angels fly up and down taking messages." Ahmed, Moroccan guide, Tangier.

CHAPTER 1
MY EYES ARE CAMERAS

Throbbing hypnagogic waves emanate from the brain centre and radiate throughout my pulsating body. The mind's flotsam and jetsam floats away like driftwood. My legs heavy as lead, burning up, my limbs locking, my muscles stiffening in sleep paralysis. I go under and a crackle of electricity pops in my head. There's a sudden jolt as I drop and catch myself falling. Sinking through my body, leaving my hanging flesh behind and the graveyard of my bones above me. I'm caught up in the strong gravitational pull of my subconscious and dragged to the lower depths by its currents, a soporific whirlpool swirling me down in concentric circles.

A fleeting fit of vertigo as I hover, teetering on the brink momentarily, before free falling into the vast, staggering, *trompe l'oeil* of the dream state. A boundless camera obscura of vague terrain and shadowy city strata, geometrically unravelling before me. Inducing that queasy disorientation of dream eyed vision, where everything is at once dizzyingly up close and far away. In your face and distant at the same time. The foreground panning back as the background zooms into focus. As I'm immersed in it, the electromagnetic force field of my soul buzzes like a hive of electron bees. Charged up like a battery, vibrating with dream power, my eyes are cameras, dreams are thinking in pictures.

The aroma of stewing tea drifts up from the all night cafe stands situated along the harbour. Carried by a crisp sea wind, it wafts like a flavoursome fog over the Portsea housing estates, just beyond the waterfront of White City, a tough, hard-nosed dockyard town on the south coast of England.

Throughout the seventies Astral Boy grew up on these sink estates, living with his mother in a cold water flat. It was a cold, empty place in every sense. An only child, his parents divorced when he was just a baby, and though he'd see his father on the odd weekend, by the time he was eleven the visits had tailed off, leading to a final, lasting estrangement. In the end it was no great shakes. Such visits amounted to little more than swapping one place of boredom and solitude for another.

His mother was a slim, attractive woman, who looked like a blonde version of sixties pop star Lulu. Stranded on an inhospitable estate, with a just a child for company, she was often lonely and hankered for male company, always on the lookout for someone to take care of her and her kid. Never stuck for an admirer, she was popular with the guys, but was a lousy picker of men. As a result, Astral Boy was forced to endure a series of asshole boyfriends, each one worse than the last, along with all the fights and rows that came with them. Such slanging matches shook him to the core, and to escape he'd turn the TV up full blast to drown it all out. When he was little he would often share his mother's bed, only to be woken brusquely in the morning and turfed out by one of these scummy, grey "uncles."

Perhaps it was doomed from the start. His mother was in labor with him for three days and nights in, what was by all accounts, an excruciatingly painful and difficult delivery. It finally culminated in a breached birth, which left his mother black and blue, and him in an incubator in intensive care for weeks afterwards. For a while there, it was all a bit touch and go. Though his critical condition eventually improved, for years afterwards he carried that incubator smell, and the grey taste of breathing tubes, in the back of his mouth and sinus. Such uncomfortable beginnings played out throughout their life together, and mother and son were never easy in each other's company.

It seemed a cosmic mistake to have been born into all this. His parents were far too young to have had him in the first place, and in later life he kidded himself that he must have been a changeling, switched for a human child, not by faeries, but by some darker, more malevolent force.

Left alone to his own devices for long periods of time, Astral Boy learnt at an early age to enjoy his own company and busy himself in solitary pursuits. As a result, books became his passports out, and one title in particular proved to have a profound influence on him, *The Encyclopedia of Witchcraft and Magic.* Back in the experimental seventies there was a fashionable revival in all things occult, and this intriguing tome had been lent to his mother by a faddy friend. When she put it to one side, uninterested in the subject, Astral Boy swooped on it, devouring its contents. It was as if the book had found *him.* Though much of the text went over his head, he was drawn to its symbols and spent hours tracing pentagrams and sigils, creating his own talismans. He learnt to chant some of the more rudimentary spells and curses, and though he didn't know it then, the book set him on the left hand path to what would became a lifelong study.

The same woman who lent his mother the book had also taken to dabbling on the Ouija board with a group of friends, and when she visited once, Astral Boy overheard her describe how an entity they had summoned kept asking after one of the participants who stopped coming to the sessions. She also related how they freaked out when the spirit of a murdered boy came through to them, chilling the room with his presence. While, in contrast, other "astrals" flew in like tornadoes, just looking to have some fun. Astral Boy got all hot and bothered at the thought of this and couldn't wait to get his hands on a Ouija board himself and start contacting some demonic spirit or lost soul on the other side.

It was a notoriously rough area where they lived, and though they owned nothing of value, their place was still targeted by burglars. After one break in, all his books and toys were stolen, and his mother became convinced a dodgy neighbour had had a hand in it. Learning this, Astral Boy placed a curse on him, and when the thieving, old lag croaked it six months later, he convinced himself the curse had worked.

The strangeness he'd felt as a kid blossomed into full blown alienation by the time Astral Boy reached his early teens. Reclusive by nature, on the rare occasions he did venture out he walked with a stoop, with his shoulders hunched and his head down. He was excruciatingly self-conscious, and when he was in the company of strangers, or even passing in front of a row of stationary cars stopped at a set of traffic lights, his face would burn up and flush beetroot red, flashing like a Belisha beacon. For years he found it difficult to even look people in the eyes, so to compensate he cultivated a 'thousand yard stare', and directed his gaze into the middle distance. As a result, people often complained he looked bored and distracted and there was some truth in this. He was always either dwelling on the past or projecting on the future, and in consequence, he rarely ever enjoyed where he was in the present.

Due to his isolated upbringing, his social skills remained undeveloped and he was not a good mixer. People were obstacles to be overcome. He struggled desperately with a lack of self confidence, and yet, paradoxically, as his precarious entry into the world proved, he could rely on his fighting spirit to get him through. With confidence however comes an underlying ease, whereas when you have to continually fight your way through life, there's always a sense of desperation lurking underneath.

As a young man this willful spirit expressed itself in more pronounced ways, particularly his appearance, and he began dying his hair and wearing make-up in honour of his boyhood pop hero, David Sylvian. Famed for his beauty, mystique and haunting music, the rarefied singer cast a total spell over him. Sylvian seemed to live an extremely cultured, glamorous and cosmopolitan lifestyle, all incredibly appealing to someone languishing in the concrete jungles of White City.

Due to Sylvian's influence, and the more vulgar and common New Romantic movement of the early-mid eighties, teenage boys, even the hard ones, could wear make-up and get away with it, such was the climate of the times. Although he cut a lone figure at school, Astral Boy was popular enough to be different and never had any problems with the other kids. The cadre of poisonous nuns who ran the school were a different matter, however, and their evil tentacles spread into every corner of student life, especially when it came to enforcing the strict dress code.

Astral Boy's repeated flouting of this code wound up getting him expelled, but he was ecstatic to leave such a drear, soulless, depressing place. You could actually feel your very lifeblood draining out of your body there. The grim, grinding tedium of it all summed up by the pithy couplet etched on a classroom desk by an old hand long gone: "Here I sit bored as hell, waiting for the fucking bell."

As soon as he hit sixteen, Astral Boy signed on to the dole, and moved into a single suite in the Portland Hotel, his rent paid by the Social. From his bedroom window he had an unbroken view of the seafront promenade. Once he left home, his relationship with his mother grew more and more distant, until eventually it fell away completely. By then it seemed much easier to burn bridges than build them.

Before he was kicked out of school, Astral Boy helped himself to a set of art books from the school library, including a biography of the American artist Edward Hopper. He had become obsessed with the artist's most famous painting, *Nighthawks*, an atmospheric and evocative composition that centered on a few lonely souls sat at the counter of an all night diner. Seen through the glass wrap-around window, and lit by harsh fluorescent lighting, the figures looked as though they were on display in some kind of human aquarium. Astral Boy fell in love with the image and tore it out of the book, hanging it on the wall at the foot of his bed, so it was the first thing he saw when he woke up every morning.

Hopper's paintings captured those frozen moments in life, of people lost in thought, in their own private worlds, in splendid isolation and reverie, experiencing the jarring stillness and melancholy that goes with it. It was a sensibility Astral Boy knew only too well and the pictures resonated with him deeply. *Nighthawks* conjured up that exact feeling of being lost and alone in the big city, and Astral Boy wished he could travel back in time and be the gaunt, spectral guy wearing the grey fedora in it. Having always felt he'd been born in the wrong place at the wrong time, he longed to have been around in New York in the 1940s, where the painting was set. He had a deep affinity for that time and place. He loved the look and style of the clothes, the men in their fedoras and sharp suits, and the sexy broads dressed in their nylons and tight pencil skirts. It was all there on show in the painting, as well as the old, film noir movies he watched on Saturday afternoons, which invariably opened with an aerial shot of the Manhattan skyline that never failed to enthrall him.

That had been an amazing period in New York, when an awful lot of the things he was into were either germinating, or taking place, like the fantastic revolutions in music and the arts. Entering through the eye of the painting, he'd wander around the city, and embark on his first, real, successful visualization. He'd visit Fifty-second Street, where genius saxophonist Charlie Parker and his Bebop comrades in arms, trumpeters Dizzy Gillespie and Miles Davis, were breaking the sound barrier of jazz. Then he'd hit the Paramount theatre to hear his favourite singer, Frank Sinatra, induce teenage riots with his mellifluous voice, bringing the whole city to a standstill with the kind of pop anarchy that Elvis and Beatlemania would replicate in the following decades. He'd hang out with his literary heroes, William Burroughs, Jack Kerouac, Allen Ginsberg and Herbert Huncke, in the midnight bars and cafes around Times Square. Through these visualizations he got to know the streets of Manhattan, virtually, but one day he'd move to New York and haunt the city of his dreams for real.

Astral Boy's early fascination with the occult deepened through his teens, developing into a serious practice. Using meditation and visualization techniques, he learnt how to concentrate the mind, and began experiencing the first of many "psychic flashes." When talking to someone with whom he had a special rapport, he'd see a short video clip of their life in his mind, revealing some personal insight, or pertinent detail, that helped shape his sense of them. He became fascinated with the dream state, and marvelled at how he'd encounter someone in a dream, weeks before actually meeting them in real life. From then on he kept a journal to record them, and over the years discovered how many of his dreams contained snatch glimpses and previews of future events, which helped explain the feeling of *déjà vous* he often experienced.

When painkillers failed to alleviate a sharp, stabbing pain in the small of his back, which had been plaguing him for weeks, he went into a lucid dream, and over consecutive nights he gave himself a deep, healing massage, and within days the pain was totally gone. Other dream premonitions emerged and he learned to live by them. One time he found out a girlfriend was cheating on him because he saw it all happening in his sleep. While a series of violent dreams, over successive nights, served as early warning signals to watch himself and be careful to avoid any physical confrontations that might come his way. He learnt to ignore such portents the hard way. After he dreamt he was being tortured and kept in an animal cage, the very next day he was suckered into a fight by some local hillbilly who didn't like the way he looked. He was usually good at skirting trouble, which in a backward, redneck town like White City came thick and fast, but he was not mindful of what had taken place the night before, and hadn't taken note of his surroundings. It was only after the violent confrontation took place, that he realised the danger signs had been there, for it happened as he was cutting through Victoria Park, a location which housed a large menagerie. It was a lesson he learned fast and never forgot again

With all the time in the world, Astral Boy threw himself into private study and set out on a drug fuelled voyage of self discovery. He thirsted for other worldly knowledge, and like all the cosmonauts of inner space before him, he was kamikaze keen to blow his consciousness wide open.

To that end, all the usual metaphysical suspects were read and digested, with most of the titles lifted from the local new age bookstore: *Confessions of an English Opium-Eater* by Thomas de Quincey, Aldous Huxley's *The Doors of Perception & Heaven and Hell, Psychic Self-Defense* by Dion Fortune,,*Journeys Out of the Body* by Robert Monroe, *Santeria Explained* by Gonzalez-Wippler, and a collection detailing the sex magick teachings and Thelemic philosophy of Aleister Crowley.

The drugs he sought were right on his doorstep too, as the bar beneath the Portland Hotel was the main hub for the city's drug scene. From the mid-eighties untill its close five years later, this grungy hole became Astral Boy's second home. It boasted a viral atmosphere, and a motley clientele, with all the teenage tribes of England on display. Punks, Bikers, Goths, and Second Generation Mods, Psychobillies and the odd stray Skinhead all hung out there. It could be an intimidating place at first, but as soon as your face got known by the regulars, you were okay. It only ever got violent when the football hooligans started getting into drugs, beause the mugs didn't know how to handle their highs.

There was also a smattering of nowhere people amongst the patrons, middle-aged marginal types, living sad, shambolic, transient lives. Human wreckage that had fallen through the cracks, left shambling from one halfway home to another. They spent their nights strung out listening to Sad Cafe records in their dingy little bedsits, and their days on an endless treadmill of dole queues, drug centres, and GP waiting rooms.

It was known that the police kept the bar under surveillance, with cameras positioned in the windows of a suspiciously empty building across the street from it, but the joint was infrequently raided. Fortunately, Astral Boy always seemed to miss the drug busts anyhow, and there was such a turnaround of fly by night landlords, you were never really

9

sure who was running the place. As the eighties stumbled on, the Portland died a slow, lingering death, until it was finally closed down by the authorities after a girl got gang raped on the pool table.

On his spiritual quest Astral Boy learnt Tarot divination, investigated Tibetan Buddhism, and read up on Astrology and the Kabbalah. These were all solo pursuits as there were no local groups practicing such studies in the area. However, he did flirt briefly with a Sai Baba encounter group, which he found via an advert on the notice board in the new age bookshop.

He had spoken to the woman who ran the group, and she invited him to visit, and a week later he was picked up by her son, Kevin, a tall, handsome young man with a dark crew cut, who came accompanied by Penny, his cute, brunette girlfriend.

The couple were so friendly they put him at ease straight away, and as they drove out to Kevin's parent's house, they each took turns to sound him out on what the evening would entail. The journey took them to the affluent, middle class suburbs of Emsworth, way out in the sticks. Taking in the fancy houses and scenery, Astral Boy could just imagine how, back in the decadent seventies, the whole area was a hot bed for swingers and wife swapping parties.

When they arrived, Astral Boy was greeted at the door by June, his warm, gregarious host, who was dressed in a long, flowing sari and sported a bindi on her forehead. Welcoming him into their spacious home, she introduced Astral Boy to her husband Harold, and two other married couples, also of retirement age, as well as Sheila, a delectable looking divorcee with a Lady Di hairdo.

Tea was served first, which gave people a chance to get acquainted, and then everyone gathered themselves in a circle on the floor to begin the group meditation. Try as he might,

Astral Boy just couldn't clear his mind sufficiently and get into it. The vibes weren't right. He'd never done anything like this in a group setting before, and he couldn't get his thoughts off Penny, whom he caught stealing meaningful glances at him. They'd taken a bit of a shine to each other. So, Astral Boy feigned his way through it as best he could, and once they'd finished, the group played him a promotional film dedicated to their Hindu guru.

Born in a small village, in southern India, in 1926, Sathya Sai Baba's divine prominence rose while he was still a youth, when stories of his alleged, miraculous powers began to spread around the region. Claiming to be the reincarnation of a beloved saint who had died eight year before he was born, he was soon heralded as the new Avatar - the latest physical manifestation of God on earth. His spiritual reputation grew internationally through the 1950-70s, and today tens of thousands of devotees came on pilgrimages, from all over the world, to pay homage to him at his ashram. Astral Boy watched as the rapturous crowd clamoured to touch the hem of the jolly, pudgy faced Godman with the wild afro, swooning as he walked amongst them in his saffron robes.

Interspersed throughout the film were several interviews with disciples who relayed how they'd witnessed the guru's magical powers, and footage was shown to prove it. Sat in front of his ecstatic congregation, Sai Baba placed his hand inside an empty clay gourd and whisked it around inside until pounds of "sacred" ashes spilt out on to the floor. He did the same trick again, only this time rice was materialised, and there were other examples shown where he seemed to conjure watches and jewellery out of thin air. To Astral Boy's mind it all looked like sleight of hand and didn't ring true, but out of politeness he pretended to be wowed by the display too.

After the video, spicy Indian delicacies were served, and there was opportunity for some chit chat. Out of character,

Zoning

Astral Boy found himself lusting after the middle aged divorcee Sheila, and plucked up the courage to go over and talk to her. Perhaps it was the attention he had been getting from Penny, combined with the sensual atmosphere, for despite his shyness, he couldn't stop checking her out. She was a bosomy gal, and the clingy, blue dress she wore highlighted the smooth curves of her voluptuous body. She was classy and well spoken, but seemed sad and disappointed and let down by life. She opened up to him, admitting how she was searching for something to give her life depth and meaning, and how looking back, she now realised how superficial and shallow her life had once been. That was before she found Sai Baba. In return, Astral Boy told her how he'd always been drawn to Eastern Mysticism, ever since he came across an illustrated book on Hinduism as a kid, full of colourful depictions of the blue skinned Gods, including Kali with her necklace of human skulls. He would've loved to have broken his sexual duck with this woman, but he could tell that, on her part, the difference in age and backgrounds was just too great between them.

The laying on of hands was offered to anyone requiring it, so Astral Boy decided to give it a go. One of the older men performed the healing, and half way through it, in front of everyone, exclaimed , "My, you're an awful worrier aren't you son?"

A musical finale brought the evening to a close and percussion instruments were provided. Everybody sat in a circle again, cross legged on cushions, and each took turns to beat out a rhythm and chant a chorus of a religious mantra to the swami. Astral Boy bottled out when it came to his turn. He was too shy and self-conscious to join in, but thankfully Harold stepped up and took his place. It was another example of how incredibly thoughtful and well meaning these nice, genuine people were. He had been treated so well by everyone. All the older males behaved very fatherly towards him and June, in particular, made a terrific fuss of him, in fact she made him feel like a young prince.

Yet, despite their hospitality and sincerity, Astral Boy remained unconvinced by their chosen one. He wondered why on earth, if you really possessed such magical powers, would you waste them on such gimmicks? Surely they could have been put to much better use than materialising ashes and rice and cheap looking watches. Plus, he found the whole cult of celebrity surrounding this "cosmic Christ" off-putting. With all that trickery, and those fawning and unquestioning believers, it smacked of that old, slave religion Christianity.

On the other hand, the encounter did leave him with a new found interest in the healing side of things and, not long afterwards, he began visiting the local Temple of Spiritualism in Southsea.

The temple itself was a modest place, situated behind a large semi-detached house, and accessed via a side alleyway. Above the entrance to the hall hung a plaque proclaiming The Seven Principles of Spiritualism: 1) The fatherhood of God. 2) The brotherhood of man. 3) The communion of the spirit and the ministry of angels. 4) The continuous existence of the human soul. 5) Personal responsibility. 6) Compensation and retribution in the hereafter for all the good and evil deeds done on earth. 7) Eternal progress is open to every human soul.

Its interior was much like any fusty church hall. Rows of cheap, tatty wooden chairs faced towards a foot high stage, draped in purple curtains. With its threadbare décor, and predominantly geriatric clientele, it evoked a yesteryear ambience. The hall had remained relatively unchanged since the 1930s, and it looked and felt frozen in time.

Though he would forego the religious services, Astral Boy did occasionally take in a seminar by a touring psychic or medium. The spiritual healing itself took place in a darkened backroom behind the stage. Astral Boy was one of the rare young faces among the temple goers, the majority being senior citizens seeking relief for their ailments. Lit only by the natural light leaking through a rear window, the room was cast in a soothing gloom. Healers hovered, dressed in white smocks, administering the laying on of hands to mostly pensioners, laid out on wooden tables, covered in a blue sheet with a thin pillow at one end.

Astral Boy used the spiritual healing to help alleviate his bouts of depression and to re-energize his psychic abilities. He always requested the healing hands be focused on his most affected areas, his head and his stomach. During one particularly powerful session, he felt his spirit being sucked up into a swirling vortex and projected out into the blackened void of the universe. There, two massive elephant tusks hovered before him, the cosmic equivalence to the entrance of a tribal village.

Astral Boy especially looked forward to his weekly chats with George, a Temple elder. George had lived an extraordinarily adventurous life, and Astral Boy loved listening to his stories and anecdotes. He'd been born in India, during the Raj, and was raised in Ceylon where he was schooled at a military academy. At the outbreak of World War Two, he enlisted into the RAF and went on to work for British intelligence. After the War he fell in love and married a glamorous dancer he met at the Moulin Rouge, and was then promoted into the diplomatic service, serving as the British High Commissioner in Rangoon.

His future seemed mapped out until he had a life changing experience while attending a seminar in Paris given by the legendary mystic Gurdjieff. With his mind fired up with new ideas, George resigned his post, and wife in tow, he toured the globe studying with Mahatmas and swamis, Sufis and holy men, secret chiefs and Native American shamans. He'd written a memoir about his epic life and travels, though it was long since out of print, and after a lifetime living in exotic climes, he and his family returned to Blighty, retiring to the south coast. Sadly, he lost his beloved wife to cancer some years ago, and now lived alone with his cats and his memories, among his souvenirs.

With his military background, and his enduring status as an officer and an old English gentleman, Astral Boy referred to him fondly as the "Wing Commander." He was still a handsome devil, with a smooth, bronzed face, twinkling blue eyes, and a shock of thick white hair, like Samuel Beckett's. These physical attributes conspired to make him look considerably younger than his years, and he attributed his rude health and sprightly demeanour to years of yoga and vegetarianism. He exuded a natural warmth and charm and when he spoke it was always in hushed, deliberate tones, that were honey to the ears.

Knowing Astral Boy had little in the way of family, George took him under his wing and became something of a mentor, answering all the probing questions fired at him. They shared a common interest in ufology, and George blew him away with his dazzling theories relating to the spiritual significance of UFOs, as well as the importance of the year in which the first UFO was sighted - 1947.

In June of that year, the first widely reported sighting of an "unidentified flying object" was made by the pilot Kenneth Arnold while flying over Washington, one of the United States of America. Arnold's description of the craft helped coin the term, "flying saucer," however, it was the events surrounding the alleged crash of a UFO in Roswell, New Mexico a month later, which got the whole modern-day UFO movement kick-started. For over the decades a conspiracy had grown claiming that extra-terrestrial entities were recovered from that downed craft, and spirited away to a top secret airbase, where they've been kept in captivity ever since by the top brass of the American military. Some conspiracy theorists have subsequently claimed that the *Stealth Bomber* aircraft was conceived and designed based on advanced technological information gleamed from these alien captives. George, however, was not entirely convinced. He put forward the more spiritual belief that UFOs first started showing up out of a cosmic concern for the planet, following the atomic drops on Hiroshima and Nagasaki. To this, he incorporated Jung's theory, postulating that the flying saucers were actually deep rooted psychological symbols, or mandalas, projections of our anxious inner selves amid the spectre of nuclear annihilation. George was vehemently anti-nukes and he explained why. Like other spiritually-minded people, he deemed the soul was an electromagnetic force field and explained that the only thing that could knock out an electromagnetic force field was the blast of an atom bomb. As a consequence, he believed the victims of Hiroshima and Nagasaki were not just destroyed physically, but were wiped out spiritually as well.

The year 1947, George argued, both marked and facilitated a paradigm shift in human evolution and consciousness, and when he ran through some of the extraordinary events that occurred that year, and laid it down the way he did, it certainly made mind-blowing sense. 1947 was the year the controversial poet and magus Aleister Crowley died, and it turned out George had met the man himself in Paris, back in the late 1930s. Unlike Astral Boy, George was not a fan of The Great Beast 666, and had little time for his blasphemous bible, *The Book of the Law,* or his self-empowering creed, Thelema. However, the subject soon led him into telling the fascinating story of Jack Parsons, Crowley's young, maverick, American disciple.

By day, Parsons was a brilliant rocket scientist whose experiments with jet propulsion would eventually help launch the American space race. By night, however, he was master of The Agape Lodge, a magickal fraternity dedicated to Crowley's teachings based in Pasadena, Southern

Californian. Between January and April of 1946, Parsons conducted the infamous magick ritual dubbed, *The Babalon Working.*

He was aided and abetted by the future founder of Scientology, L Ron Hubbard, who scried the aethyrs while Parsons ritually summoned an elemental or supernatural being into his life. She duly arrived in the alluring, otherworldly guise of Marjorie Cameron, a flame haired, natural born witch, who was destined to become his wife and Scarlet Woman. During their love making, Parsons invoked Crowley's sex Goddess Babalon, and drew her spirit down from the astral plane to incarnate her in Cameron's womb. His dream was that Babalon would rise up to overthrow the tyranny of Judeo-Christianity and, once victorious, usher in Crowley's revolutionary neo-pagan credo. The requisite nine month duration for this, truly "phantom," pregnancy meant a projected birth date of early 1947, and although George remained skeptical about it he did contend: "Who could refute that the second half of the twentieth century was far more Babalonian than the first?" As a footnote, the Wing Commander alleged that the "Enochian calls" or angel language, originally discovered by the Elizabethan wizard John Dee, and used by Parsons and Hubbard in *The Babalon Working,* was actually the lost language of Atlantis.

George was a walking encyclopedia of esoteric knowledge like this and, during another arcane rap, he hipped Astral Boy to the legend of Lucifer - *The Light Bringer* - the most beautiful and wise of all God's angels. Contrary to the conventional view of him, George held that Lucifer had been cast out of heaven for showering forbidden knowledge and enlightenment upon humanity, against Jehovah's wishes, who wanted mankind to remain mentally enslaved to him. In one fanciful strand of the story, George told how, as leader of the Watcher angels, Lucifer swooped down with his rebel angels in tow, and had sex with the humans and animals on earth. This cross breeding of Gods and mortals creating a semi-divine race of giants like Cyclops, while the celestial/bestial union produced mythical creatures like the Centaur, the Minotaur and Pegasus. From then on Astral Boy began to view Lucifer as the original iconoclast, a James Dean anti-hero rebelling against the father figure. He invoked his name during his magickal rituals, and drew upon him for sustenance and inspiration.

The masterful way in which George seamlessly segued these interconnected events into one, long, fascinating flow took Astral Boy's breath away, and if nothing else, it certainly made history more interesting. George cautioned that it was not wise to discuss such revelatory matters with just anyone however, and urged him to remain tight lipped about them in mixed company. Astral Boy was at that impressionable age, and George's libertarian thoughts and occult beliefs informed a great deal of his thinking. Sometimes, like when it came to the matter of crime and punishment, the two were interlocked. George preached an eye for an eye philosophy, and argued that if somebody crossed you or did you wrong, you had the total right to use whatever magickal means at your disposal to avenge them. This was music to Astral Boy's ears. Perhaps, George taught, if people knew that such bad behaviour carried the severest punishment, they might be more circumspect in their dealings. He took an equally unequivocal view when it came to the deteriorating state of society, particularly the sadistically violent, scummy substrata responsible for the most heinous crimes. George maintained the only way to end such atrocities was to introduce eugenics and stop "this rubbish breeding rubbish."

Astral Boy dug the healers. They were good people. Kind, caring, gentle folk, either ethereal, white haired old ladies or venerable, soulful gents like George. As in any organization, however, such qualities were not universally held. A few years later, when Astral Boy moved to South London, he scoured the local spiritualist chapters and was disappointed to find that they were mostly a dismal lot, running shabby dens of egotism and rigidity. One deluded dingbat openly bragged about how he was channeling an entity from Andromeda, while the authoritarian head of another branch got up on his high horse and chastised him for admitting he enjoyed an occasional drink and smoke. Astral Boy didn't take kindly to that. Not only was this a rude and patronising tone to take with a stranger, but to him the attitude reeked of yet more religious dogma and spiritual abstinence.

Astral Boy's friendship with George ran from his late teens into his early twenties and, looking back, he felt they'd purposely met so that the Wing Commander could counsel and guide him through to the next stage of his life. Before he left White City and moved to London, George gave Astral Boy an Abraxas charm in the form of a gold ring as a parting gift. Abraxas was a Gnostic deity and an ancient source of divine emanations, who symbolized the reconciliation of good and evil, light and darkness, and the transcendence of them both. The ring bore Abraxas' image on the front, and with his rooster's head, man's body and serpent legs, it was yet another in the celestial/bestial God line. He was always depicted wielding a whip and bearing a shield, symbols that were both powerful and protective, and its likeness had been worn as a talisman since Roman times to avert illness and ward off evil spirits. On a personal level, George said the ring symbolised Astral Boy's transition from boyhood to manhood, and it also served a psychometric purpose, enabling him to feel his mentor's presence wherever he went.

Throughout most his teens Astral Boy was a confirmed asexual, and though he had chances at school, the thought of sex left him cold. His sexual libido didn't kick in properly until later, and by that time he had already cast off on his voyage of drug fuelled discovery, which suppressed any sexual stirrings that may have been loitering in his loins. In time, Astral Boy would crave sensual gratification in all its forms and, slowly but surely, he was being inexorably drawn away from Spiritualism into chaos and sex magick.

Besides his weekly visits to the Temple of Spiritualism, Astral Boy rarely left his hotel room, other than to make the rounds of the drug dens and shooting galleries dotted along the seafront. These high-ceilinged flats were occupied by a rogue's gallery of watery eyed, hollow cheeked loners and misfits, blaring a non-stop soundtrack of Bob Marley. You'd leave one apartment at the start of one of his songs and arrive at another pad at the end of it. Astral Boy's favourite drug of choice was the amphetamine Dexedrine, commonly known as *Dexys*, the pills having inspired the band Dexys Midnight Runners. Back in the late eighties you could score four of them for a quid and six would fix you all night. The Dexys sharpened Astral Boy's mind and helped fuel his three and four day magick rituals and visualisation sessions. He'd then crash for a few days and would have to endure the god-awful come down that came with it. Greeting the chill of dawn, his insides gnawed by a gaping emptiness.

Astral Boy's moniker came courtesy of his drug buddies who christened him with it, one night, after he blabbed about the out of body experiences he had earlier in his childhood. The sarcastic nickname sealed his spooky reputation and stuck with him from that moment on.

His first experience happened when he was five years old. His mother had taken him on a ferry trip, across the harbour to Gosport, to visit his grandfather, who worked as a bosun on a cargo ship moored there. The old man actually lived on the boat with a skeleton crew, and Astral Boy's sole memory of him was of eating ice cream as they watched TV together. He died soon after.

Later they visited Gosport Park, and while his mother

sunbathed, Astral Boy wandered off, bucket and spade in hand, to a nearby pond. It was a small, circular cauldron, only fifty feet in diameter, which had been excavated in the middle of a concrete picnic area. He watched a pair of swans as they sailed serenely across the surface, and at some point, his plastic bucket found its way into the water. For some inexplicable reason, as he was unable to swim, he went in after it. Whether he fell in while trying to retrieve the bucket or just jumped in after it he couldn't be sure, the motive was lost in the mists of time. Whatever the reason, Astral Boy sunk like a stone as soon as he hit the surface. Submerged, he was astounded to find he was watching himself drowning from a parallel position about twenty feet away. He gazed, enthralled, as his body descended in slow motion, while the rays of dappled sunbeams illuminating the watery murk, lent the underwater setting a shimmering, dream-like quality. He felt a serene tranquility as he marvelled at the extraordinary sight, only to be snapped out of it abruptly, as he felt himself being dragged up through the water. He was now back in his body and, looking upwards, he could just make out two black, blurry rings. These dark circles soon came into sharp focus as he broke the surface of the water and found they were the eye frames of a pair of spectacles worn by the mustachioed man who was saving his life.

As if this near death trauma wasn't enough to stomach, he then had to suffer the humiliation of being dragged to a nearby cafe by his mother, where he was fed hot soup by the pitying owners, and made to wear a dress belonging to their daughter while his wet clothes dried off.

A year later he found himself experiencing it all over again. After complaining that he couldn't stand the hallway light in his eyes, his mother panicked and rushed him to hospital, fearing he was suffering from meningitis. As a whole team of doctors and nurses fought, unsuccessfully, to pin him down long enough to administer the lumbar puncture, he drifted out of body, and from a vantage point high up in the corner of the ceiling, he observed the whole marathon struggle going on below him. He fretted as he watched himself resisting the painful procedure, and was relieved when the doctors and nurses finally gave up. A good thing too as it turned out to be a false alarm.

For years these mystifying experiences stayed with him, lingering in the back of his mind. It wasn't until he read a book on the paranormal as a teenager, and found out about astral projection, that it all began to make sense. A well documented phenomenon, astral projection was sparked when a person's spirit was propelled out of their body, either when they were close to death or during moments of immense suffering and pain. Astral Boy learned how certain individuals had managed to astrally project at will, and were doing so as "pilots" on astral air force programmes, "remote viewing" for intelligence agencies like the KGB and the CIA. Astral Boy vowed that he too would learn such skills and master this technique.

CHAPTER 2
WHITE CITY

Looking out from the glass bottomed hull of the Mothership at an aerial view of the concrete jungles of Somerstown, White City. The ominous hum of the spacecraft resounds inside the fuselage.

Below, there are three L-shaped housing estates that back onto one another, each a four-story maisonette block, with a pedestrian concourse running between them. At the heart is Oldbury House which stands as like a backward 'L', a mirror image of Stratford House just beside it. Longbridge House is located above them, a building dwarfed by the seventeen-story high Leamington tower block that stands adjacent to it. There is a children's swing park nestled beneath the tower block, and beyond a dual carriageway lies White City's Guildhall and Town Centre.

Every ground floor flat on each estate has a modest little

23

back garden, with a tiny flowerbed. The back gardens are enclosed by a railing fence, which are themselves bounded by a patch of grassland. Dotted on the grasslands on each estate are large, raised brick planters, with bushes and cherry blossom trees. Three are also three small separate rose gardens located at the outer hinge of each L-shaped block. Each backs onto the side wall of a walk-through alcove that allows exit and entrance to the maisonettes, via stairwells.

Rotary washing lines twirl on the forecourts of the Oldbury House estate. Across from it, separated by the resident's car park, is Halesowen House, which contains only eight flats in all, four on each floor. Rearing up behind it, across a one lane road, is the looming presence of Skyrise Block, Leamington's most brutal twin tower. Two long, rectangular bin sheds bookend the car park. During chases, the local kids run across these rooftops, scrunching the gravel firing beneath their feet. Three residential garages are housed in the middle of the larger bin shed, but they are owned by outsiders not affiliated with the estate. With all the menfolk at work, the car park is generally deserted during the day, so the neighbourhood kids use it as a football pitch, utilising the middle garage as a goal. This causes consternation amongst some of the elderly tenants, who complain about the almighty, cymbal-like crash the ball makes smashing against the aluminium garage door when a goal is scored.

Situated across the road from the estate is The Robert Peel, the local pub, a low level building with smoke tinted windows and a carport in front. A knee-high brick wall surrounds the car port, and follows the bend of the road which winds 'round in front of it.

To the south of Oldbury House, across another one lane road, lies the neighbourhood youth club. A deceptively small building, it houses a table tennis room upstairs, as well as a rec room and gymnasium below, which is used for both sports and discos. An alleyway at the rear of the club leads out onto a concrete five-a-side football pitch, bounded on the street side by a high wire perimeter fence, and on the opposite side by the towering, back wall of the old, disused distillery. Two movable iron framed goals stand either end. One, up against the side wall of the youth club, the other pushed up against the rusting wire fence of the derelict cold storage yard next door. A little beyond these immediate boundaries, the streets begin to bleed into Southsea, the seafront part of town.

A balmy summers afternoon, bathed in sparkling, seventies sunshine, the clouds like fluffy white tire tracks in the sky. 10CC's *I'm Not in Love* plays out from an open window over the Somerstown Estates. A mile up in the sky above, the mothership hovers, monitoring the small electrical substation, ensconced at the rear of the youth club. There, ranging in ages between eight and thirteen, a rag tag gang of neighbourhood kids, known locally as the Skyrise Muthas, lounge over the battle ship grey electrical transformers. Dangling his legs over one of the cooling fins, Skyrise Kid savours the deep, vibrating hum of the transformer as it buzzes through him. He's a blonde, feather haired twelve year old boy, with a baby face that makes him look even younger.

After a while, they move over to the shady grove opposite and infest the acorn trees. The sound of stick-fighting can be heard, emanating from the window of the kendo class taking place on the top floor of the community centre on the corner. The boys begin taunting the name of the psycho dog belonging to a curmudgeonly, old recluse who lives in a top flat overlooking the trees. As the boy's call it out of its lair, Skyrise Kid stands teetering on the four foot high railing fence that girds the grove. He's trying to make yet another unsuccessful attempt to join his comrades in the tree tops. Jumping from the fence onto the tree's lowest bough, he hooks his arms and legs around it and tries desperately to pull himself up. Unfortunately, being younger and smaller than the rest, and decidedly weaker in his upper arms, it's an arduous process and his strenuous efforts result in a grueling, tiresome impasse. While he manages to lock his arms and legs, he cannot summon enough strength to pull himself up, so he just ends up hanging there, upside down, until his arms and legs grow weary and he loses his grip, and is forced to hang drop to the ground.

He is just about to scale the fence one more time when the psycho dog emerges from the narrow alleyway running between the community centre and the block of flats. In slow motion each one of the Skyrise Muthas turn their heads as the animal rounds the corner. Still preoccupied with his climb, Skyrise Kid is the last to see the dog coming. He is only alerted by the frenzied ravings of his pals in the trees who shake the branches like hysterical monkeys, screaming at him to run for it.

Seen in slow motion from street level, Kid glances over his shoulder and looks askance as he finds the unleashed dog gunning for him. Stranded in no man's land, he tears away from the railings and takes off. Viewed front on, his wan face becomes a harrowing portrait of panic and desperation. His eyebrows arched, his eyes as wide as saucers, as he hares it down the street heading for Oldbury House.

At this point the dog is about twenty feet behind him, but gaining, chewing up the ground between them. As he sprints, a sickening cocktail rush of fear and adrenalin saps at his legs, weakening and draining them. The hollering from the Skyrise Muthas following the chase becomes a jumbled row in his ears, and yet as he bolts past the entrance of the pub car park, Kid can distinctly make out the fretful sound of the dogs claws scratching on the pavement behind him. Tears stream down his face as he feels the animal bearing down on him and realises he's not going to make it home. He chokes up, distraught and watery legged, his heart pounding in his chest, hammering in his head, his throat sore, his mouth raw from the run. Just as Kid steps off the curb the barreling beast plows into him. Kid slams face first onto the asphalt and feels a shocking sting of pain as the dog's fangs puncture and sink into the soft flesh on the back of his thigh.

FLASH CUT: A microscopic image of blood coursing through veins and arteries.

FLASH CUT: Bacteria spreads through the blood in a Petri dish. The blood is fouled.

FLASH CUT: Fragments of torn childhood photographs flutter across a wasteland.

FLASH FORWARD: In an attic room, a now teenaged Skyrise Kid cranks a hypodermic syringe into his vein with a slow burning sting, a musky stench of Astral dogs fumes off his body.

FLASH BACK: Kid lay in a crumpled heap, winded and shell-shocked. He felt violated. The attack had knocked the slats out of his system, it was so real it was unreal. Strange thing was the moment the bite was inflicted, the dog seemed to lose all interest in him and wandered away. Struggling to his feet, Kid was brought back to consciousness by the sound of mocking laughter. Looking up he found two boys from the neighbouring Stratford estate, sitting astride their *Chopper* bikes on the other side of the road. They were pointing at him and chuckling, having witnessed the whole attack. Kid squirmed with embarrassment and felt his face burning up. He hobbled home mortified and humiliated. As he reached the mouth of the Oldbury car park a mind-warping mist descended in his head, like heat vapours rising off a hot, desert highway, and he blacked out, collapsing on the concrete.

Throughout the late 1970s-80s, the Mort family lived in a ground floor flat in Oldbury House. They weren't so much a family as a bunch of lost souls living under the same roof. Kid spent most of his teens living there, sharing the house with his bedridden nan, his sad, reclusive, gay uncle, Ryland, his sweet natured, put upon aunt Babs, and her daughter Gemma, his younger cousin.

After a short period away, living on his own, Kid returned home again and stayed there while he was strung out on drugs, and in and out of the detox clinic and rehab center. He was in a bad way. He'd been diagnosed as suffering from Hebephrenia - "teenage schizophrenia" as his psychiatrist explained it to him, a psychosis brought on by his LSD use. He'd been prescribed *Chlorpromazine Largactil*, a heavy duty tranquillizer, usually only administered to terminal schizophrenics, to help diffuse the flashbacks he was having. Since the breakdown he'd been plagued by panic attacks and needed to be in a safe place where there were always people on hand in case he hyperventilated.

The detox and rehab had done no good. It was down to him now. After some soul searching he realised that as he had brought this condition on himself, by the same token it was down to him to rid himself of it. Mercifully, his state of being was self-induced rather than inborn, and besides, the thought of spending the rest of his life stranded on a nut ward in one of those grim, Victorian mental hospitals scared him straight. So Kid came home to his family, sleeping on a mattress on the floor of Babs' and Gemma's bedroom. His family rarely, if ever, congregated together, each choosing to live in self-imposed exile, cooped up in the solitude of their own bedrooms. They each had portable televisions in their rooms, so the living room downstairs went mostly unused. Ryland forbade guests anyway, particularly at night, and there were many embarrassing scenes when he had come downstairs to rudely show the kids' friends the door. It was a horrible, lifeless, stagnant atmosphere to live in, and loneliness leaked from every room.

There was also an uncle whom Kid and Gemma had never met, a soldier who'd been stationed over in Northern Ireland in the early seventies. During his stint there, he'd met and married a catholic girl and then disappeared. The family had heard nothing from him in twenty years and it all seemed an incredibly murky business. Rumour had it that he switched sides or fallen foul of the paramilitaries. Press reports at the time suspected foul play and spoke of a cover up by the authorities, but no one really knew for sure.

Nan had been a bit of a girl when she was younger, who had certainly "depended on the kindness of strangers," but she was a zombie now. She still had the burn marks on her temples from the electroshock treatment, and she'd been operated on so many times that scars riddled her stomach like ugly, purple zippers. Kid remembered sitting outside Nan's ward during one hospital visit, and overhearing a loose-lipped nurse referring to how they "opened her up and she was rotting inside." The words conjured such an awful, indelible image. It was one of those things you hear once and can never get out of your mind again.

Now Nan just lay there in bed, smoking and staring at the wall like a mental patient. All the adults in the household chain-smoked endlessly, but Nan had a dangerous habit of falling asleep with a lit cigarette in her fingers, and her nightgown and blankets were pock marked with burn holes. The last time she left the house they found her wandering the streets barefoot, picking up dog-ends. Thank God those days were over. She was hopelessly addicted to prescription painkillers like *Distalgesic* and *Halcyon* sleeping tablets. Pills and cigarettes were the main currency of the house, and their consumption led to running battles and all kinds of skullduggery. One time Kid woke up to find Nan hunched over him, searching his bedding for his own pills. Caught in the act, she cracked a guilty, gummy grin, which was both pathetic and obscene, she then bullshitted that she was looking for some *Benylin* cough medicine. However grotesque, it was the first time he'd seen her smile in years,

29

and though angered and appalled by her pilfering, Kid was tickled deep down that the sly, old girl still had it in her. Still, when he chastised her for it later she just looked at him with those blank, vacant, hollow eyes and sighed, "I'm hooked," in her soft, Scottish brogue. The resignation of her admission cut him to the quick. There was no answer to that.

With his feint freckles and short, copper coloured hair, parted on the side, Kid's downward spiralling uncle retained a school boy quality that belied his age and dishevelled appearance. Despite his fuller face and middle aged spread, his uncle's hairstyle and manner reminded Kid of the camp comic Kenneth Williams, though his eyes wore the same, tired, world weary expressions of another aging actor, Dirk Bogarde, at his most pensive.

A homosexual from the old school, Ryland voted Conservative, loved the Royal Family, and enjoyed watching such traditionally manly pursuits as golf and cricket on television. There were only flashes of his gayness while he was sober. He'd blurt out queer, Polari sayings like, "Bona dear bona" or "Omi-polone, seems like a nice boy," and when Kid asked him for a drag of his cigarette, he would deliver the withering riposte, "Drag my arse around town."

Both mother and son loved the Machiavellian JR Ewing character in *Dallas,* and a poster of the dastardly fiend, grinning wickedly beneath the brim of his Stetson, hung on Nan's wall at the foot of her bed. When they weren't watching telly, they leisurely made their way through the pile of paperbacks they'd amassed over the years, bought from charity shops and jumble sales. Stacks of them stood in columns against the wall at the foot of the stairs.

It was from his uncle that Kid picked up his own reading habits, as well as his reclusive tendencies. Although permanently unemployed, Ryland did all the housework, cooked most of the meals, and on the sly, took a series of twilight jobs, either cleaning or cheffing in local pubs and restaurants. It was always nightshifts or early morning work, and this brought him little or no social contact with others. Ryland was completely cut off.

He had little in common with the young queens he occasionally saw on television, and when White City did eventually get its first gay pub, Ryland wound up feeling as alienated and out of step there as anywhere else. Like his mother, Ryland was also hooked on prescription barbiturates, but what made it worse was he mixed them with vodka, and the alcohol brought out his nasty, violent side, as well as his tortured, psychosexual proclivities. The toxic combination turned him into a real Jekyll and Hyde character, he could be a total swine, and he frightened and upset the kids no end. On more than one occasion, Kid was forced to fight off his drunken uncle's hot, molesting hands.

What originally began as Christmas benders, increased over the years, until his drunken binges became ever more frequent. More often than not, they became a prelude to his mysterious, nocturnal excursions, with the alcohol acting as rocket fuel, propelling him out of the house. Kid and Gemma were left wondering just where he went on these nights out, and somehow the word "cottaging" filtered down to them, a word, which to their naive minds, conjured up an image of their uncle thatching roofs. It was only later that they learnt what he was really doing, checking out other men's cocks!

Ryland usually wandered down to the dockyard, cruising for matlows, but wherever he went the outcome was invariably the same. After coming on to the wrong guy, or group of guys, he'd receive a good kicking, and the children witnessed firsthand what the results of a queer bashing looked like, when he returned home in the wee small hours, his face battered, covered in blood and bruises. One time, when he did actually manage to lure a fella home, Babs refused to let them in, so Ryland punched his bloody fist through the front door window. Another memory Kid could never forget, was his uncle's first suicide attempt. Kid came downstairs in the middle of the night and found him, slumped drunk in a chair in the kitchen, a bread knife in one hand, a geyser of blood spurting from his slashed wrist.

Kid's long suffering aunt Babs, on the other hand, couldn't have been more different. She was a kind, bonnie-faced woman with a roly-poly frame and a heart the size of Africa. She was a much put upon woman, and food was one of the few pleasures and comforts in her life. She longed for love, but had been let down badly, countless times. Her long, brown hair fell all the way down her back, and the smock dresses she covered herself up in exaggerated, rather than concealed, her rotund carriage.

Her daughter Gemma was born out of wedlock and went through life never knowing her father. Two years Kid's junior, Gemma was a winsome, auburn haired waif with a pale, washed out face. Though cousins, they grew up together and fought like brother and sister, serving as convenient punchbags for each other's anger and frustration. It was only many years later, in retrospect, that Kid learnt how Gemma's eating disorder began, because she was convinced Ryland was putting pins in her dinner and trying to poison her.

Babs was the glue that kept this horror show together, and it was a thankless task, having to put up with an ailing mother, a hateful, suicidal brother, a troubled daughter and a kicking junkie for a nephew. It was *she* who had to swab Nan's septic stomach with saline, *she* who fished Ryland's head out of the oven when he tried to gas himself, *she* who accompanied Kid to the hospital after another overdose.

As if this dogs life at home life wasn't joyless enough, she then had to go to work at her betting shop and deal with all the dregs of humanity that darken a bookie's door. An endless procession of inveterate gamblers and losers, who'd blow their week's pay packet and then think nothing of taking out their anger on her. She was paid peanuts and treated like shit, but Babs soldiered on, day in day out, with the whole soul-destroying grind. She put up with it all and remained unbroken and unbowed, but she would have given anything for a quiet life.

She won the odd victory though, getting one over on her firm by working a little scam on the side. Her most ingenious shanghai occurred when a punter approached her window to place an accumulator bet, only to find he'd left his money at home. Instead of voiding the slip, Babs put it to one side and waited on the result. The accumulator came in, paying out big time. Babs paid for the bet out of the winnings and pocketed the rest. Another time, a punter put a bet on the prestigious French Prix de l'arc de Triomphe horse race. Unbeknownst to him, the trainer of the horse he backed had a "coupling," meaning he had two horses in the same race. A bet on one of these horses meant a bet on both, so if one lost and the other came in, the punter would have a double chance of winning. The dopey prick didn't realise this, so when his horse lost he screwed up his betting slip and threw it on the floor. Babs clocked him and waited until closing time, when she retrieved the slip and copped the loot.

With Babs at work, and Gemma at school, days would fly by with Kid, Ryland and Nan tucked away in their bedrooms, all stoned out of their minds, either asleep or monged out in front of the telly, their curtains drawn on a sunny day.

At the beginning of the nineties, the family moved out of Somerstown to the Canberra House estate situated on Arundel Street, near the centre of town. It was a return that brought them full circle back to the Landport area, where they'd all once lived back in the early-mid-seventies. It was not long after this move that Ryland's lethal cocktail of pills and booze finally took its toll, and got the better of him once and for all. Babs found him one morning, lying on his side, exactly the way he always did when he was watching television. Except this time his eyes were closed, his face was purple, and his head was propped up on a clenched fist. His body was already stiff with rigor mortis.

Kid was residing in Morocco at the time; he was finally free of drugs, and was making a living starring in porn films. When he heard the news he didn't feel much sadness, actually he was kind of relieved. He knew how despairing his uncle had been, trapped in a hopeless life with no future prospects, now death had released him from that terminal misery. For some people there was no way out, there was only a dead end, and Ryland had hit his.

CHAPTER 3
SKYSCRAPER PARK

Boosted by the publication of some album reviews, and an editorial promise of more paid work to come, Astral Boy left White City in late 1991 and moved to London to pursue a writing career. He rented a small studio flat in Du Cane Court, an Art Deco apartment block on the Balham High Road in South London. According to local legend, Hitler had earmarked the grand complex as a future headquarters for the SS, had the Nazi invasion panned out. It had previously been home to many famous music hall stars back in the 30s, and the basement was filled to the brim with tables and chairs, dressers and wardrobes belonging to former tenants who had either died or moved away without them. The furniture was free to new occupants to help furnish their rooms, and rummaging around one afternoon, Astral Boy unearthed an old Ouija board table which he quickly spirited upstairs.

Zoning

In only a matter of months, Astral Boy blagged a job writing features for *Hustler* magazine, and on the side he freelanced as a music journalist. On the strength of his rap reportage, he landed his first paid travel assignment to America. The trip took him to New York, his dream city, to interview the rap star Ice-T, who was currently embroiled in a political shit storm ignited by his incendiary track *Cop Killer*. The rapper was in town to shoot a video and play a gig with his band Bodycount, and although Astral Boy was only budgeted to be there for three days, he'd already planned to extend his stay on his own dime, and use the opportunity to visit the Psychic Research Center in Manhattan, renowned for its studies into paranormal phenomenon like astral projection and ESP.

He had been corresponding with its director, Professor Sergei Litvinov, for the past six months, having initially written to him detailing his personal history of out of body experiences. His letter piqued the professor's interest, and he sent back an open invitation to visit. Finally, at last, Astral Boy was getting some validation. The professor's pedigree was high. He was a renowned expert on parapsychology, including astral projection, and had written extensively on the paranormal and the occult, authoring two highly acclaimed biographies of his fellow Siberian countrymen, Gurdjieff and Rasputin. His letter of invitation stated how he was looking to recruit some volunteers for a new remote viewing project and, on paper at least, Astral Boy seemed a perfect candidate.

The flight to New York took eight hours but flying didn't bother him. Astral Boy felt as safe and secure on a plane as if he was sitting in a comfortable armchair at home. However, after savouring the euphoria of takeoff the rest was a bore, so to kill travel time he knocked back a 100ml of Valium and decided to see what his dreams had to offer. He had a window seat fortunately which meant he wouldn't be disturbed by the passenger next to him begging for the toilet, and he requested the stewardess not to wake him for his in-flight meal. He closed his eyes and waited for the tablets to take hold. As his body numbed, Astral Boy used the hypnotic technique he'd learned in regression therapy. He imagined himself walking slowly down the thirteen steps of a spiral staircase, counting down each one as he went. As he mentally stepped off the last, bottom stair he felt his astral body plunge into the void, sinking to the fathomless depths of his subconscious.

Over the next six hours a blizzard of dreams flooded his mind, almost feverish in their intensity, but alas, nothing memorable enough that he could really hold onto. For despite his best efforts, his sleep cycle was repeatedly broken up, interrupted by the noise of his surroundings, including the turbulence warning aired loudly over the intercom. His dreams got lost and scrambled in the process as he drifted up from the REM stages of sleep. It didn't matter much anyway, for the final dream installment that unfolded, just before he woke up for landing, was a real doozy that eclipsed all that had gone before it.

Obviously inspired by the journey he had undertaken, Astral Boy found himself staggering in pixilated steps through the entrance of a Nissan car plant, situated on an industrial estate on the outskirts of White City. A fleet of identical cars line the expansive forecourt in front of the company's HQ. The premises are deserted. Maybe it's a Sunday, or the offices are closed for a bank holiday. Astral Boy wanders into an adjacent field behind the facility where he finds a hand held camcorder. Looking through the viewfinder, his hand swings wildly up to the sky to reveal a jumbo jet, a thousand feet up, hanging motionless in midair. The plane is fixed in a nosedive position, frozen in its final stage of descent. It just hangs there suspended, as if its progress had been halted by some omnipotent hand activating the pause button on a remote control.

Zoning

Back on the ground a gentle breeze rustles through the outlying trees and hedgerows, but suddenly the peace is shattered by an ear piercing roar of engines, and the camcorder veers up to capture the reanimated plane as it plummets to earth. A scorching sound rips the sky like a torn sheet. Astral Boy runs for cover, skidding down a grass embankment, the earth slippery beneath his feet. He trips and falls face first into a shallow ditch. Spread out on his stomach, he feels the earth rumbling beneath him as the aircraft crashes in a nearby field with an almighty boom.

Once the shock and tremors subside, an unsettling lull sets in, and for a brief moment all is tranquil again. Then the faint sound of rotor blades cutting the air is heard, way off in the distance. Its resonance increasing in volume, gradually at first, then swelling to a crescendo, like a trillion boomerangs returning. Astral Boy curls up into a ball and covers his head, as the ruptured sky empties a deluge of debris that showers the sodden grass around him. The projectiles hitting the ground in a series of galloping thumps. When it all seems to be over, Astral Boy gets to his feet and finds the whole area littered with batteries and lighters fallen from the sky.

The flight arrived in New York around midnight, the witching hour. Astral Boy marvelled at the magnificence of the Manhattan skyline below. The skyscrapers lit up like Christmas trees, the red, neon streets glowing like hot molten lava burning through the cracks of the city. For the first time in his life he felt like he'd come home.

The sweet, chrome scent of *Joop* cologne lingered in his midtown hotel room, left over from the previous tenant. Nightwalking the charged, narcotic streets - he got a contact high just from being on them - Astral Boy was amazed by how deserted they got at night. You could walk whole blocks of this teeming metropolis, inhabited by millions of people, and not see a single soul. The city was just a vast movie set. The sidewalks, fresh from recent rain showers, glistened under the orange haze of streetlights, the skyscrapers as broad and impressive as Robert Mitchum's shoulders.

He loved the dark, urban splendor of it all. The streets pounding and resounding with knuckle dragging, head nodding, hip hop beats, a visceral, reverberating soundtrack that encapsulated the environment perfectly. A rolling montage of subway cars, afterhour storefronts and graffiti tags plastering every spare inch of wall space. It was as if rap music had been purposely created just to define and compliment this city, just as jazz had fifty years ago. The music fitted the scenery, it put you there.

After checking out Times Square, Astral Boy hung a right and spent a couple of hours cruising the strip joints, grindhouses and porno stores in the vice blocks on Forty-second Street, the sexual excitement flipping over in his stomach like a Mexican jumping bean. As he approached the Port Authority Bus Terminal he became aware of a big, fat blob of a black guy, about his age, tracking him as he walked. He had peeled off from a gang of shady looking lowlifes hanging on the corner up ahead, and now seemed to be zeroing in on him. With his barrel belly, cherubic face and broad, welcoming smile, he seemed more cuddly than threatening. Still, as the punk stepped to him, Astral Boy tensed up, readying himself for whatever came next. The cat laid his customary hustle on, "Hey wassup? Public Enemy, my man, what yo dig?" The dude had clocked the PE emblem on Astral Boy's baseball cap. "I'm cool, man," Astral Boy muttered, keeping his head down, trying to walk on. But the motherfucker blocked his path, and the initial friendliness of his opening gambit evaporated as he got all up in his face with his shit.

It all went down so quick. Action is always faster than reaction, and in that split second his assailant got the jump on him. Before he knew it the scumbag was snatch grabbing at his crutch and pants, looking for money he guessed. Caught off guard, Astral Boy spun round defensively and unleashed a hail of punches at the knucklehead, only to find that his arms were weighted and numb and he couldn't muster any power in them. It was as though he were punching through water. By the time his fists actually made contact, they had become limp and ineffectual and made no impact at all. His shots just sunk into the punk's soft, blubbery belly, buffeted by the flab. When the tub of shit managed to trap him in a bear hug, Astral Boy's fury turned to all out panic. He abhorred bodily contact, and the revulsion of feeling enveloped by all that revolting flesh, not to mention the vile stench of the fat fuck's body odour, triggered one last-ditch, all out effort. Summoning all the remaining fight and strength he had in him, Astral Boy managed to break his stranglehold and flee, leaving the piece of shit standing dumbstruck in the middle of the street.

With his insides tremoring with fear and adrenalin, Astral Boy hightailed it out of there, running like gangbusters down Ninth Avenue, heading for Hell's Kitchen. Watching him flee, an enigmatic smile broke across the mugger's face. He erupted into an uproarious laugh, flashing gold fronts, then turned and gave a "what the fuck" shrug to one of his homeboys lurking down the street, a sly eyed Puerto Rican hood slouched against a wire fence.

Astral Boy kept running until he came to a vacant car lot. Confident he was safe enough and out of harm's way, he cooled his jets and pulled up exhausted, gasping for breath. The altercation left him shook up and deeply upset. He was both unnerved and incensed, stung by his own sense of powerlessness and vulnerability. Amid the confusion, Astral Boy subliminally sensed that something incriminating had been secreted on him, and as he doubled over, hands on hips, trying to catch his breath, he felt a strange, tickly irritation in his ass. Under the sombre glow of a street lamp, he unbuttoned his jeans, lowered his drawers and dug his fingers into his rectum. Using his thumb and forefinger, he fished some kinda dragonfly out of his ass, he could just make out its crumpled wings and tail-like body in the half-light. Astral Boy knew instinctively that once the insect gained entrance into his system it would lay inside the gut and gestate, feeding off the food waste and fat deposits until it grew large enough to hatch and burst out of his stomach.

Japanese cartoon characters form in the cloudless blue sky above the traffic lights outside White City's main train station. Warring armies build up exponentially, multiplying from themselves like Russian nesting dolls. Medieval samurai spring out from jack in the boxes, dashing in their long, pleated battle dresses. Flying banshees swoop in with swords drawn, diamonds glinting in their eyes. The whole Technicolor sky alive with Manga.

The movie camera capturing this phantasmagoria drifts away and floats over to the Somerstown Estates nearby. It cranes up the grey-faced exterior of Skyrise Block, halts when it reaches the seventeenth floor, and tracks right, zeroing in on the last flat at the end. The focus blurs as it enters through the heavily netted, doubled glazed windows.

Inside, the scene is set for torture film. Huddled in a semicircle, in a white walled room, bare of furniture, are hooded worshippers of Tabeth Ali, the mythical leader of an ancient death cult. Their faces are obscured, but their eyes are cast down upon the sacrificial slab of a man, ritualistically displayed before them. He is laid out on a medieval rack, fully naked, with his identity concealed behind a bondage mask. His feet have been gaffa taped together, and his arms are bound above his head. Judging from the multiple lesions on his doughy flesh, they had really done a number on him, and it looks like they raided the toolbox to do it.

From the inflamed rope burns around his neck, to the

weeping lacerations across his gut, legs and chest. God knows how long he's been put through this, but some of the dark bruises are now yellowing around the edges. His nipples are singed and charred, and surrounded by ash from stubbed out cigarettes, while his mutilated genitals are caked in dry blood, and have fag ends sticking out of the scrotum. Flanking the victim on either side are two donkeys, standing docile, facing in opposite directions. Surrounding them are six Astral dogs, their hackles raised, their ears pinned back, their eyes transfixed on the proceedings. The high priest of the cult lifts his arms above his cowl and performs a benediction. He then barks a command at his fellow cultists, and the creepy cabal step back away from their human sacrifice, passing the dogs, primed and ready to pounce, awaiting the signal.

As soon as the disciples disappear out of camera frame, the scene immediately erupts into action. The dogs go ballistic, attacking the animals ferociously from all sides. Some lock their powerful jaws onto the donkey's haunches, while others claw the hides from their withers. The mules try to buck and rear, braying in distress, but a close up shows their hooves have been chained to the floor, so as they struggle to kick out they lose their footing and buckle forwards on their fetlocks. One of the donkeys is brought down with blood gushing from its muzzle, its ears tattered and chewed. The other slumps onto its side, its hocks torn, its muzzle battered, the flesh flayed from its head so its skull is now showing.

Overwhelmed by the savagery, the donkeys are soon vanquished, and the dogs get to feast on the messy, purple innards that spill out on to the floor with a foul, steaming sizzle, the stomach lining dangling like red ribbons and bloody rags. As they feed on the ruptured bellies, loud, squelching noises emanate from the Astral dogs jowls, then there's the succulent sound of joints being wrenched from their sockets, and teeth crunching up bones. The dogs growl at each other as they fight to wolf down the last of the abattoir slop, licking their bloody chops once they're done sniffing over the entrails.

Throughout the pandemonium the stricken snuff star has been wriggling and thrashing about, struggling to break his confinement, agonizingly aware of the onslaught going on around him. Now, as the pack advance, he judders violently as if in the throes of an epileptic fit, his belly wobbling, the roar of his strangled screams stifled by the gag over his mouth. An alarming close-up of his masked face captures his terrorized eyes straining through the slits, searching the ceiling, unable to settle on a fixed point, all too aware of the excruciating ordeal to come.

The dogs swarm and clamber onto their hysterical quarry, the white surroundings highlighting the sheen of their shiny, black coats. The beasts swiftly lay waste to him, slavering over the man's corpulent carcass with crazed, orgiastic relish.

Gradually the camera pulls back away from the gore fest, withdrawing from the room, out through an adjacent hallway, the tumult declining as it does. The camera retreats until the picture slowly fades to black. It reopens a few moments later, backtracking off the apartment's impregnable front door. It looks like a bank vault, metal-plated with chrome tubing and one of those air lock wheels you see on submarines. The image lingers momentarily to communicate the detail that nothing can be heard going on inside the flat from outside it.

Down on the twelfth floor, a fourteen year old Skyrise Kid loiters in the hallway with his homeboy Bronx, waiting for the doors of the elevator to open. Bronx is a mixed race kid, named after his black American sailor father who abandoned him and his white mother after he was born and returned home to New York. As soon as they enter, Bronx punches the emergency stop button, and using a makeshift crowbar, they jimmy open the hatch on the roof of the car. Kid then cups his hands and gives Bronx a boost and he springs up and pulls himself through the hatch. Once he's up there, Kid flicks off the emergency hold and presses the button for the ground floor. Bronx then reaches down, and with his strong arms, pulls Kid up to join him, the silver doors closing as Kid legs disappear. Like a pair of miscreants their eyes light up, amped with delinquent excitement. Kid can't stop his right leg from shaking at the thought of the impending kicks to come, and he bites his lower lip in anticipation. He shows Bronx the lining in the fly of his gangbanger jeans which bears the legend "blow me" embroidered in gold stitching. Bronx cracks a devilish grin, and as their elevator drops with a jolt, they begin *ridin' the 'vators.*

The lift shaft walls that whoosh pass their faces are plastered in graffiti tags, enshrining the names of Skyrise Muthas past and present. Names like *Basso* and *Duce,* and the one they call *Duetski.* The boys look down and watch as another elevator car travels upwards to meet them. They ready themselves as the two cars converge, and then leap onto the roof of the ascending lift which whisks back up to the gods. They strike surfer poses as they disappear into the darkness, screaming hysterically and pissing themselves laughing.

To carry this out you really had to be bang on with your timing, a careless lack of concentration or a mistimed jump, and you risked dismemberment or instant death. Tragically, such a fate befell a couple of their friends. Kid could still remember how the crushed skull of one pal left a crumbly slick of blood and scrambled brain matter smeared down the back wall of the lift shaft. His other mate was a little luckier, he survived, but lost an arm and suffered a broken neck. Still, as he recovered, he wore his injuries like battle scars, bestowing a nickname on them, *The VATs* - Vator Action Tractions. Inevitably, the authorities stepped it and modified the elevators, putting an end to their dangerous, daredevil stunts.

CHAPTER 4
WHERE DO THEY COME FROM,
WHERE DO THEY GO?

The Psychic Research Center was located on the top floor of New York's famous Flatiron Building. It seemed only fitting that such pioneering work was being carried out in what was once the first skyscraper ever built in Manhattan. The Flatiron Building was where, back in the day, the slang term "23 Skidoo" derived. Due to its triangular design, and its position at Twenty-third Street on the intersection of Fifth Avenue and Broadway, unusual wind currents would swirl around the building at ground level, and lift the skirts of the broads walking by. Word soon got around, and cops had to be deployed to disperse the peepers, hoping to catch a flash of ankle. They would do so by hollering, "23 Skidoo" at them.

Astral Boy was well aware that the number twenty-three

held a great deal of mystical significance. Thanks to George, his head was filled with the stuff. In chaos magick it signified random chance, the guiding principle behind Brion Gysin's and William S. Burroughs' cut-up technique. Burroughs himself had his own individual take on the number, observing that it was often associated with tragedy and disasters. In Aleister Crowley's cosmology the number symbolised "a parting, a removal," and similarly the key phrase of hexagram twenty-three in the I Ching meant "splitting apart." In UFO lore, it was the number of the original Annunaki aliens who seeded human life on spaceship earth. Some theologians believed that two thirds was the percentage of angels who decided to stay loyal with God in heaven, while the remaining third sided with Lucifer and fell.

Actually, Astral Boy had already had a dose of symbolism that very morning. There was something warm and cosy in the colourisation of American television, and he was in the habit of sleeping with the TV on at low volume, as it helped him get off to sleep. As fate would have it, he'd woken early to find a favourite film playing, *Bell, Book and Candle,* a romantic comedy about a coven of witches set in beatnik era Greenwich Village. The film included a scene in which a bewitched, bothered and bewildered Jimmy Stewart kisses witch Kim Novak on the roof of the Flatiron Building. It was a nice touch of synchronicity. The Gods were smiling.

Astral Boy rode the elevator to the twenty-second level, where the Psychic Research Center took up the entire top floor. The doors opened onto a reception area where a frizzy haired girl, with a "kill me" expression on her face, sat behind a desk. A pyramid emblazoned with the initials *PRC* hung on the wall above her.

Astral Boy gave his name and explained he had an appointment with the Professor. The receptionist said okay, then picked up the phone to confirm his arrival with, he presumed, the professor's secretary. He declined her offer to take a seat and gave her a meek smile she didn't return. There was no call for this offhand manner. He couldn't abide rudeness. The shitty attitude continued as she buzzed him through the security door with nary a word. God, the bitch was misery on a stick.

"Up ya ass with broken glass.... may your soul be raped by demons," Astral Boy murmured under his breath as he pushed on through.

On the other side of the door he was met by an emaciated, hawkish looking woman with a sallow, skeletal face and tortoiseshell tinted hair. She was weirdly striking. It wasn't just her waxy complexion, but her spidery eyelashes and impossibly blue eyes, contacts he guessed. She introduced herself as the professor's personal assistant and they shook hands. Dressed in a blue pantsuit that revealed her bony breastplate, she certainly looked the part, and in a brusque, businesslike manner she led him down a warren of corridors. The atmosphere seemed vacuum packed, as if all the air had been sucked out of it.

He wondered if the scrawny woman was anorexic, she was so painfully thin. Anorexia was a touchy subject for him. Although he hadn't suffered from the disorder, it put him on edge. He just couldn't handle the subject. The merest mention of it on TV and he had to change the channel. Perhaps it was some residual trauma from a past life. Anyway, back in the day, thirty odd years ago, she had probably been a real looker, but time does terrible things to women's faces. Her powdery soft skin was lined with wrinkles and crow's feet, and she had a withered top lip - a tell tale sign of female aging. There was something rotten about her too. Astral Boy had an aversion to strong odours and she had a particularly offensive one, a pungent, unpleasant mixture of garlic, moth balls and sperm. There was also a whiff of a cult about her. Having picked up on her Scottish accent, Astral Boy asked how long she had been living in America. She glossed over this, and instead gushed about how her work with the professor, which had taken her all over the world. Astral Boy pegged her as a guru groupie. He imagined her as a cute hippie chick back in the sixties, searching for someone or something to give a meaning to her life. He fantasized that she had been in one of those brainwashing cults like the Moonies, or been a member of the shadowy Process Church of the Final Judgment. He pictured her in a black cape, preaching about the unification of Christ and Satan on the moneyed streets of Mayfair or the head shops of Haight-Ashbury. He bet she had a trepanning hole in her head, and he wouldn't be at all surprised if she'd escaped from Jonestown just before the big sleep was dreamt up.

On the way to the professor's study, she pointed out the chambers where the remote viewing experiments took place, and Astral Boy caught a brief glimpse of the room through a porthole window. It looked like the flight deck of a spaceship. "The walls and floors are lined with felt to keep the orgone energy in," she told him, for no apparent reason. Finally, they reached the professor's study, and the woman knocked on the door, waiting until a voice said, "Enter." She let herself in, and announced Astral Boy's arrival, then beckoned him inside. As Astral Boy entered, the professor rose up from behind his large mahogany desk to welcome him. They shook hands, and by the time Astral Boy had sunk into the sumptuous, leather armchair offered him, the woman had already left. He drunk it all in. The study was part library, part antique shop, with rows of bookshelves, swish furnishings, expensive artifacts and degrees and diplomas papering the walls. The man himself was an eccentric looking old duffer, dressed in a crumpled, three piece suit with a bald, egg shaped noggin, rung by a nimbus of bushy grey hair. He had sad elephant eyes, drawn and lined with heavy bags under them. In fact, he was every inch the classic model of a mad professor, except there was nothing dusty about the subjects *he* was interested in.

After a friendly preamble, the professor started talking about the numerous projects the Center was running, and they discussed Astral Boy's eligibility as a test subject for the new remote viewing programme they were undertaking. It was then that Astral Boy noted the print of Hopper's *Nighthawks* on the wall. He gave a smile of recognition which the professor picked up on.

"Have you seen the original?"

"No, but it's been a favourite picture of mine for as long as I can remember."

"The original's in Chicago. It's a lot smaller than you'd imagine."

"Yeah, I bet, they always are."

The professor rose from his seat and moved over to the painting. Instinctively, Astral Boy got up and followed him. The prof continued the conversation.

"Y'know, Hopper was dubbed an American realist... but on the contrary, his work is actually highly stylised."

"Yeah, it's weird, a lot of his work does nothing for me. He did a whole series of seascapes, with lighthouses, sail boats and cottages off Cape Cod, which are so chocolate box. It's hard to believe they're by the same guy who painted such a masterpiece as this."

"Yes, I suppose they make good jigsaw puzzles."

Astral Boy laughed and then leaned into the picture.

"I think this city brought out the best in him. I love all the paintings centered on New York, like *Drugstore, New York Movie, Office at Night.* His dames are sexy too."

He was trying to impress him and the professor smiled, then peered back at the frame.

"But there's an unease there also, something ominous and sinister just lying beneath the surface."

Astral Boy gestured at the figures in the painting.

"I think anybody who's spent time alone in a bar or a café, wondering what the hell they're doing with their life can relate to it. Some people think the characters are lost or caught up in their own world, but if you look I think there's something definitely going on between the redhead and the mysterious looking fella. She's definitely invading his personal space."

"She's looking for a pick-up maybe?"

"Yeah, you can just imagine Rita Hayworth playing her in a film.

"Yes. Viewed from a distance it looks like a still from a film."

"In one of the books I read, it said the painting was a big, stylistic influence on the film noir movies, but I don't think it was painted until 1942, and I think they were already making film noir movies by then."

"Well, Hopper and his wife we're both avid moviegoers, so it's entirely possible. Perhaps the influence was going both ways."

Astral Boy picked out the spectral figure at the counter.

"I always thought that guy looks like William S. Burroughs."

"Ah yes.... his *eminence grise*."

He wasn't sure whether the professor was referring to Burroughs or the enigmatic figure in the painting. The professor pointed to the diner itself.

"Can you see the curve in the glass front? It has the same architectural shape as this building,"

"Yes, I noticed. That's why I thought you liked it."

Professor Litvinov nodded and smiled again. He then turned away from the picture and moved back to his desk. Astral Boy trailed him and they both sat back down.

"I read somewhere that the painting was meant to based on a joint Hopper saw on Greenwich Avenue," Astral Boy continued. "I was gonna take a walk down there later and see if I can find it."

"Well, good luck….."

Astral Boy got the message. The professor wanted to move things along.

During their conversation, Astral Boy found out the professor was also conducting group therapy sessions for people caught up in the whole alien abduction phenomenon. This little detail threw him. Astral Boy had no idea the professor had an interest in ufology, and at once he launched into his Wing Commander inspired rap about the significance of the year 1947, and all the momentous events connected with it. Professor Litvinov seemed impressed and smiled knowingly, nodding throughout. When his rap ended the professor rose from his seat, and wandered over to the window. Gazing up wistfully at the sky he sighed: "Where do they come from? Where do they go?"

Matters were brought to a close once plans were made for Astral Boy to return the following afternoon to run some tests. But before leaving the building there was one, last curious incident. It was the damnedest thing. As Astral Boy walked down the corridor, heading back to the reception area, he realised he had left his umbrella behind in the professors study, so he turned back to collect it. Not thinking, he re-entered the office without knocking and broke in on the professor unexpectedly, who was deep in conversation with his assistant. Strangely, he seemed to be talking in a straight English accent. Caught unawares, their faces dropped for a moment, and in the blink of an eye, Astral Boy witnessed the professor's kindly demeanour evaporate, as a dark cloud passed across his face. Then, without missing a beat, the professor slipped back into his Russian tongue, and the pair play-acted their way out of it, as if nothing had happened. The charade was so convincing it left Astral Boy wondering whether he'd imagined the whole thing. After apologizing for his intrusion, Astral Boy retrieved his brolly and exited in silence, relieved to get the hell out of there.

Caught in the viewfinder of a Super 8 camera, a UFO hovers over the Somerstown Estates. The shaky picture shows a stingray-shaped craft with a long tail, surrounded in a halo of red light. At its nerve centre are what appear to be flickering orange flames. However, a close-up shot reveals a hive of electro activity, like amber tinted TV static. "Centrifugal force," Kid overhears someone say later. The camera is unable to keep track of the craft as it darts all over the place, zigzagging at unrecordable speeds, zooming in and out of frame, changing direction, turning on a dime. The UFO first appeared floating silently above the electrical substation at the rear of the youth club. The Skyrise Muthas were the first to catch sight of it, as its arrival broke up their five-a-side football game. They chased the craft as it slowly hovered east over the estate, heading in the direction of the swing park.

When they arrive there, the kids find a chandelier shaped mothership twirling majestically in the sky above them. Residents from Longbridge House and the Leamington Tower block hang out of their windows, hollering and pointing up at it, they just can't believe their eyes. A collective gasp goes up from everyone as the ship swoops down suddenly and whooshes over their heads, shattering into six separate UFOs. There was a classic, fifties style, hubcap flying saucer. A black, rather sinister, wafer thin, triangular craft with lights pin-spotted on the three corners of its undercarriage. There was a cigar shaped craft and one that looked a rotating wagon wheel. A canister shaped spaceship with a dull grey patina, and lastly the sleek, futuristic, pewter coloured stingray UFO, that Kid and the others had chased originally. It appeared that each alien spacecraft could contract and expand at will, because they do so. They zip around the vicinity, performing a bewildering aerial display, alternating their trajectories like an insect in flight with omnidirectional flight manoeuvres that completely defy and confound the laws of aeronautics. Actually, it looks as if they're showing off.

Kid runs home to tell his family all about it, but as he bolts through the side door entrance to Oldbury House, the suction from a UFOs tractor beam seizes his chest and hoists him off the ground. Instinctively, he reaches out and manages to grab a hold of the frame above the door, leaving his body flailing, and his legs peddling in the air. There must have been a technical malfunction in the craft, because, momentarily, the tractor beam loses its juice and relinquishes its grip. Sprung free, Kid swings through the open doorway, like a gymnast propelled off the high bars, and flies into the stairwell where he's unceremoniously dumped on his ass, the door slamming shut behind him. He hoped that the surrounding walls would sap the tractor beam's strength, and protect him from its effect, but as he went to open the connecting door to take him out onto the landing, he felt its suction brace his chest once more as it tried to hoover him up again. It was like one of those nightmares where you try to run but find your legs are paralysed to the spot. Kid tries to weather the force, lunging and thrusting himself forward, until he's leaning, like a ski jumper, into the wind. But the grip on the soles of his shoes gives way and, losing his footing, Kid slips and falls face forward. He is then sent tumbling backwards like a skittle, and is knocked out unconscious when he cracks his head open against the metal plated door sill.

Asked later by a TV news reporter to describe what he had seen, one of the younger Skyrise Muthas looks into the camera and says, "It looked like a spaceship, exactly like a spaceship."

As Skyrise Kid lay unconscious in the stairwell, the first floor landings of Oldbury House transform into a rickety pontoon made out of bamboo cane. Row boats and gondolas are tied to its moorings. The estate is now flooded, *a la* Venice, and enveloped in a sweltering, oppressive, oven heat. A lake covers the car park and frontcourts, its oily black waters lit by a full moon. When Kid comes to, he is changed from twelve year old boy into a nineteen year old youth. He gets into a boat and casts off, reeds and bulrushes snapping under the bow.

It's like the opening shot of a movie. His eyes are cameras that skim over the azure, Mediterranean waters, and then sweep up, rising high over the sea walls, to scan the panorama of Tangier beyond. A vast, elevated monorail system stretches across the full length of the Tangier beachfront. The fifty foot high construction is supported by white, concave girders, shaped in Philippe Starcks' impossibly sharp, signature style. The train ferries passengers to and from the port into town.

She was standing in the corridor of the train, outside the first class compartments, looking out the window at the passing landscape. As Kid approached he instinctively dropped his eyes, but having already caught a blurred impression of her, he was compelled to get a closer look. Under the guise that he too was taking in the scenery, Kid stood next to her and followed her gaze, trying to catch a sly glimpse out of the corner of his eye. He was careful not to gawp and make her feel even more self-conscious then she already was.

She was like a Max Ernst fantasy made flesh, a real, living, breathing Chimera. A half woman, half bird grotesque, both visually compelling, and more than a little off-putting. He could tell how aware she was of her freakish facade by her forlorn, abject persona. Her lonely isolation expressed through all too human eyes. When, at certain times, she swivelled her feathery head, or was physiologically impelled to peck at the air with her beak, those caged, timorous eyes would scour those around her, anxiously checking to see if the embarrassing affectations had been noticed. Kid's heart went out to her, yet at the same time there was something diseased about her.

Kid went back to the pretence of studying the passing landscape, which rushed by all a blur. That was unless he fixed his eyes upon a particular passing object, like a Eucalyptus tree or a wooden fence. Then the subject would come into sharp focus, the speed of its movement brought to a momentary standstill as he held his gaze upon it. Then, once he let go, it would disappear, flung back into the distance. As they stood alone in uncomfortable silence, Kid sensed her arm extending, and moving down slowly towards his. He squirmed inside as he felt her sharp, pointed claw grip his soft palm. It a weird, unsettling sensation, the stark contrast between her rough, brittle talon and his soft, pink flesh.

The moment they touch, they're transported to the shabby back alley where his hotel is. The alley is set on a steep incline, like all the streets leading up from the beachfront. There's a derelict shack at the bottom of the alley that has fallen into disuse. It has rusty bars where the front door used to be, and its faded green shutters have blanched over the years due the unrelenting sunlight. A heap of rubble is piled up against the wall on the right, it's mostly plaster that has cracked and peeled off the weathered walls, corroded by the moisture from the damp sea air.

In the midst of this run down scenery, the bird woman appears. Playfully, she chases two Alsatian puppies, who bound around excitedly, their tails wagging. The creature sweeps the pups off the ground, gathering them in her arms. With her talons under their backsides, they sit up on their hind legs, their spines resting against her chest, baring their fluffy, blonde bellies. With her sharp claws she brushes aside their wavering tails and expertly draws back their furry foreskins, exposing their raw, pink, lipstick cocks. Gently, she coaxes the skin back and forth, gradually building up momentum, until she is masturbating the dogs with gleeful frenzy. The puppies pant, paws up, their tongues licking her lovingly under her chin.

Astral Boy sat in the departure area of the Port Authority, waiting for the ride out to JFK Airport to catch his flight back to London. The surroundings were far from salubrious. Whack jobs and crazies roamed the waiting area, and he made sure to stay out of their way. You got the impression that it would only take a wrong word or some flashpoint to set one of these ticking time bombs off, and they would explode and take out half the people in the place. One of them, a beat, old, black geezer with a grey goatee, limped across the concourse, dragging a lame foot behind. He looked haunted and ravaged, and as he passed in front of him he jabbered to himself, "Do it for the kids, gotta do it for the kids."

He had to get high. Departure time was still an hour away, so Astral Boy cut out to the john. The place stank of tramps. He locked himself into a stall, put the toilet lid down, sat and sprinkled his wrap of heroin onto some silver foil. He lit up and chased. A killer rush fucked him up and his head fell back against the wall. He sat there stoned for a while, staring into space, breathless in the euphoric afterglow. Then he got a strange inkling. Something told him to look inside the empty casing of the toilet roll dispenser, and peering in, he found a pentagram with the numbers 666 written on a pyramid in the centre of it. What would possess someone to draw that? He thought to himself. What a strange place to… his thoughts trailed off, blindsided by another headrush.

Inspired by the drawing and the drug, Astral Boy wrote a smack poem on the cubicle wall.

DRAGONS

Locked in the thin prison, my lungs become its lair.
Wrapped up in ashy skin, emblazoned nostrils flare.
Blows me up like a balloon, curls the ends of my toes.

Slip the skin, win my wings, as the blood burns in my nose.
Fire in your belly, smoke drifts to the ceiling.
Now your stomachs sated, now you're really seeing.....
DRAGONS

There was still some time to kill, so Astral Boy slid into one of the special waiting room chairs that had a coin operated, mini TV box mounted on it. Twenty-five cents bought fifteen minutes of viewing time. With a gloved hand he wiped the film of grime off the TV screen, and fed two quarters into the slot. He switched the dial and surfed through the channels of late night television, stopping to catch the tail end of a jailhouse interview with Charles Manson. At one point, Astral Boy tuned to a channel that was just static. He gazed at it awhile, spaced out, remembering what George had once told him, how television snow was actually photon energy caused by the radiation left over from the Big Bang fifteen billion years ago.

The smack made him itch like crazy, and left him scratching his face and sides, feeling like a chimp with ticks. No wonder they called it having a monkey on your back. As fellow passengers drifted across his periphery like dark, shadowy ice flows, Astral Boy nodded out and slid into oblivion. The sound from the television set igniting images in his mind's eye.

He clicked over to The Oprah Winfrey Show. To the polite applause of the audience, two exotic Polynesian girls walk onto the stage and take their seats on the high, backless stools. The teenage twins wear traditional, Polynesian dresses, the floral prints a riot of colour. Oprah sketches in the background information surrounding them. Born identical twin sisters, on a remote Hawaiian island, the girls are looked upon as Gods by the local inhabitants, due to their fantastical powers. They have been invited onto the show to demonstrate these powers, and it's the first time they have ever been performed outside of their native land. Oprah asks the cryptic, prearranged question, "What do you think of Hiroshima?"

Over a hushed, expectant silence the twins respond to the question by slipping into a deep, hypnotic trance. Suddenly, they begin speaking in tongues, their high, fluted voices intoning an ethereal, melismatic mantra. The strange words swirl around their heads in a carousel of sound, their resonance decreasing in volume as they travel behind their heads, increasing again when they come back round. This strange incantation of an ancient, esoteric language seems impossible to locate, though every so often a recognisable word will stand out momentarily, before it all flounders back into incomprehension.

Abruptly, the chant is broken, and simultaneously, as if on cue, the twins' eyes roll back into their heads and the possession takes hold. The girls are rocked violently by some volcanic inner turbulence. They struggle, battling to release the grappling entities rifling around inside them. All of a sudden, ectoplasm erupts from their mouths with a loud, throaty roar, spewing forth gooey, white strands that float weightlessly up to the ceiling in one, long, billowing flow. It looks like silvery gauze is being pulled out of their mouths. The heat from the studio lights turns the ectoplasm into a candy floss material.

Ever so slowly, the twins levitate up from their chairs until they hang suspended in mid-air. Gasps of disbelief flood forth from the rapt studio audience. Two dusky female assistants approach the stage from right and left. They are also from the same island, and have worked with the sisters many times over the years. They remove the stools from beneath the twins, and place them to the side of the stage. They play their part and go through their paces, completely oblivious to what's going on, having seen it all before.

The twin on the left spins herself upside down, so that her

toes now point to the ceiling and her long, black hair hangs to the floor. Gracefully, she rotates back into a bolt upright position, but then, miraculously, her body starts separating. Incredulous moans of "Jesus" and "Oh, My God," greet this bizarre display, as the stunned, stupefied audience struggle to take in and comprehend what they are witnessing.

This latest development creates a complete state of confusion in the control room, with the programme director and vision mixer scrambling to decide which cameras to cut to in order to capture the best shot. For viewers watching at home, the television pictures swing about wildly for a moment, and there's a rushed frame of the polished studio floor and the cables trailing behind a camera that swings around for a close up of a rattled female audience member who has her hands to her mouth. She looks on, utterly transfixed as the twin separates her head from her shoulders, and then her body from her legs. There are no breaks and each segment just hovers in the air. Attention then turns to her sister who is still intact, until a shaft of light breaks through an opening in her midsection and her entire body collapses in on itself. She turns herself inside out, and the trunk of the body remerges as a crustacean's exoskeleton, the green shell glistening under the bright studio lights. Her remaining arms morph into red lobster claws.

Meanwhile, the segmented body parts of the twin on the left shrink down and transform into a chrysalis. As if shot by time lapse photography, her head emerges out of the cocoon, but she now has a pelican's bill and a gular pouch flapping beneath it. The bill snaps at the air, as the rest of her body materialises, transmogrified into the thorax and abdomen of a caterpillar, her arms replaced by an enormous set of insect wings that hum as she buzzes around the studio.

The whole mystifying exhibition sends shock waves of panic and hysteria through the audience, and staffers are deployed to help pacify and settle them. Others remain understandably speechless, struck dumb by it all. Oprah herself is captured, standing behind the cameras, looking on open-mouthed, flabbergasted by what is unfurling before her. The show fades out to a commercial break.

Returning, a now composed Oprah introduces Professor Litvinov, whom she describes as a specialist on the paranormal from the Psychic Research Center in New York. A caption pops up confirming his title. Astral Boy can't believe the Prof's wearing a toupee. Even worse, the ill fitting wig sits on his head skew-whiff and doesn't jive with the salt and pepper grey of his natural hair, so he looks really goofy. Regardless, the professor suggests that the twins' power is not dissimilar to that of a poltergeist, and explains that their apparent ability to manipulate matter comes from their expert harnessing of electromagnetic energy.

Oprah explains that the twins have left the building now, and that despite requests they shun all interviews. But in their place she talks to their younger sister, a cute, bubbly teenager sitting in the front row, who shares none of her siblings' otherworldly prowess. Oprah asks her what it's like having such strange, gifted creatures as sisters, and the girl recollects how, as children, the twins would spend prolonged periods of time "mirror gazing" in their bedroom. She describes how she once snuck in on them while they were in the middle of their scrying, and saw how their hands had turned black and in place of fingers they had long, white tendrils. She also relates how she enjoys watching them fly about, and as she speaks footage of the twins from an old home movie is played on the screens in the studio. The silent, colour film shows the twins as little girls, fluttering around in the air, encircling each other in the sky above a sun-drenched beach. Though their human heads are visible, their bodies have transformed into an exquisitely beautiful pair of speckled winged butterflies.

CHAPTER 5
THE ALIEN CHILD

It was a kinky set up, right up his sleazy alley. Skyrise Kid knocked at Dirty Sue's front door, one of the many stoneclad houses in the backstreet behind the Kings Theatre in White City. They had met a fortnight earlier at a *grab-a-granny* night in one of the nightclub dives along the seafront, opposite the pier. His stomach fluttered with sexual excitement the moment he laid eyes on her. Tanned, with smoky eyes and a shag of dishwater blonde hair, her voluptuous body was squeezed into a tight, figure hugging, Lycra dress that accentuated every ample curve of her body. Most noticeably of all, she was endowed with the biggest set of tits Kid had ever seen. Man, she was stacked! Although, without make-up, she had one of those rough-hewn, working class faces, she knew how to make the most out of herself, and once she was all dolled up and had the war paint on, she was earthily glamorous. In fact, with her raunchy looks, pneumatic physique and wanton demeanour, she bore a striking resemblance to the buxom, seventies porn queen Candy Samples. She even wore one of those black, silk ribbon chokers, or "porno collars," as Kid dubbed it, so beloved of those smut stars of that era.

She was a bubbly, vivacious woman, somewhere in her late forties/early fifties, a boon for Kid who had a thing for older women. There was a particular sexual frisson between an older woman and a younger man that was just delicious, and Sue was a strapping, super sexy example of it. Her alluring, come to bed eyes, were full of sexual promise, and the flirty, suggestive looks she gave with them helped inspire Kid's pet name for her, "Dirty Sue."

He meant it affectionately, and she took it in good humour. Hell, if nothing else it was accurate. Her lewd and lascivious behaviour was off the charts, and in the end it was an easy pick up. There was an instant sexual attraction between them as soon as their eyes locked on. They both knew what they were out for. Sue later confided how she thought Kid looked foxy and dug his long, blonde hair. She was tickled to have bagged herself a twenty year old, and Kid made sure to refer to her as "girl" a lot, cos she lapped up. It made her feel eighteen again. They clicked right off, and spent the rest of the evening dancing and chatting at the bar. Though it transpired she was married, Sue claimed it was an open relationship and, furthermore, boasted how she was something of a superstar on the swingers circuit and amateur porn scene. That night, Kid teamed up with a buddy and dragged her back to his seafront flat for a nasty little three-way. They fucked her ragged. It was carnal and animalistic and Sue really got the cum flying. As a finale she sucked them both off, and they shot their loads over her humungous tits. Sue responded by massaging the cum into her tits, coating them in a sticky, glacial sheen.

Afterwards, when they were alone, Sue told him about the

porno business she and her husband had set up. Reacting to the boom in real life amateur porn, they began making their own tapes which proved so successful they now had a lucrative distribution deal with a film company in London. Her husband was getting on a bit and couldn't get it up so good, and so instead he got his rocks off, voyeuristically, by watching her make out with a string of young bucks, and that's how Kid ended up here today.

Sue came to the door dressed to thrill, with a naughty twinkle in her eyes. She looked scrumptious. Beneath an unbuttoned business suit she wore a low cut top, its plunging neckline displaying her lush, abundant cleavage to full effect. Her short, black pencil skirt was slashed up the sides, showing off her luscious legs, encased in sheer black stockings. A pair of black patent stilettos completed the slutty secretary look. Once the door closed, Sue kissed Kid full on the mouth and "hmmm'd" with delight, giggling after as she wiped her lipstick off his lips. She was heavily made-up; this was for the cameras Kid later realized, and bathed in musky perfume. Kid breathed it in as he kissed her and nuzzled her neck, savouring the intoxicating scent that was like catnip to him.

The doorway led straight into the living room, a model of clean, homely domesticity. A three piece suite was angled inwards towards the television in the far corner, while the focal point of the room was a large, wooden ship's wheel that hung on the wall above the fireplace. A carriage clock and a ship in a bottle sat on the mantelpiece, and the nautical theme continued with naval plaques, framed photographs of sea liners and portraits of tall ships adorning the walls. The old man's obviously an old sea dog, Kid concluded to himself, as he took in the mannish surroundings.

Sue had previously mentioned that her husband was a gun enthusiast, and beneath the free-standing stairs Kid found a handsome collection of them in a glass display cabinet.

The handguns and the cabinet were kept under lock and key, however two Western rifles hung crisscross on the wall above them. Kid was a pretty decent shot himself and had once belonged to a local gun club, which he visited once or twice a week, on the outskirts of town. It was run out of a casemate, one in a series of cavernous bastions that had once been used to store armaments and munitions during the Second World War. There was something magical about shooting guns. Using a gun you could project your will and cause change to occur over a great distance. He remembered the first time he ever shot one. Many years ago he had been taken to a farm in Kent, run by family friends, and one of the teenage boys had allowed him to fire off a rifle. Kid watched in wonder, as in the far off distance, his shot tore a branch off an apple tree. It felt God-like and he was hooked. It was a pure visceral thrill. Kid wanted to keep the branch as a memento and as they approached the tree they found that all the fallen, rotten apples were infested with wasps. Being kids they stomped on them, and it felt real satisfying, crushing the apples and beasties into a mushy pulp.

The living room had a bar set up along the far wall, stocked with an array of beers and spirits and even a soda syphon Kid hadn't seen since the seventies. He noticed that Sue had got him a bottle of tequila, his favourite tipple, and before he knew it, she'd fixed them both a drink. They sat next to each other on the sofa and, between sips, they started canoodling. That was, until Sue's husband entered the room. He walked up to where they were sitting, extending an outstretched hand and a warm greeting.

"Hi Kid, I'm Geoff, pleased to meet you."

Kid rose instantly to his feet and shook hands.

"Hey man, er, yeah, pleased to meetcha," he replied, a little on the back foot.

As they sat back down Kid intuitively moved to an armchair, allowing the man of the house to sit with his wife on the sofa. Balding, with a paunch and a brownish beard, flecked with grey, Geoff's less than impressive appearance, along with his personable and above all *passive* manner, put Kid at ease. It came as quite a relief because he still felt a bit weird about all this, coming round here just to quench the insatiable appetite of his hot, horny wife. However, the guy seemed genuinely happy to have him there and, after some gun talk, Geoff was soon avidly regaling him with X-rated stories concerning their recent sexsploits at the Hedonism resort in the Caribbean. He even got out the snap shots they had published in *Hustler's Readers Wives* section.

While Kid looked through the photos, Sue got up to replenish their drinks, and this time she brought him back a bottle of Mexican beer. In her absence, she shed her jacket. She was obviously hotting up. She sat there, next to her husband, giving Kid the eye, as her hubby waxed lyrical on pornography.

"Sex is an itch and pornography scratches that itch," he told Kid, who nodded in agreement. The guy obviously fancied himself as a bit of a connoisseur.

"The key to pornography is the way it blends the most beautiful aspects of the human animal with the most debased. Erotica is pretty lies, pornography is ugly truth" he pontificated.

Kid got into it a bit with him.

"Whenever I watch those old porno tapes, like those old, seventies *Swedish Erotica* loops, I always wonder about the women, where did they come from? Where did they go? I wanna know what they're doing now and where that house is where the scene's being shot."

"Well, most of those American ones were made in the Bay Area near San Francisco, not LA like most people think," Geoff explained.

As the porn talk continued Kid couldn't help riffing.

"I'm really hooked on those enema tapes. I used to wonder

what people meant when they spoke about getting a religious experience from taking in those big, baroque fountains in Italy, and then I watched an enema tape and BOOM I got it, I understood completely. It *is* a religious experience."

Geoff didn't get Kid's screwy humour, but he smiled politely. Perhaps if they knew each other better. Geoff then started bragging about the contacts they made on the swingers scene.

"Sue told me you've got an interest in, what shall we call it, exotica? Y'know we can get our hands on practically anything."

"Like what?"

"Well we've gotta little ring going, just among a select group of friends. We swap films, and pass 'em round. There's bondage tapes, gangbangs, some kinky stuff y'know. One guy's gotta whole load of vintage erotica, peep show loops and stag films from the 1920s and '30s, featuring all these flapper girls fucking in sepia which is just great."

Kid was only half listening, his attention distracted by Sue's saucy shenanigans. For as her husband spoke she sat there, teasing him, crossing and uncrossing her legs, flashing him brief, tantalising glimpses of her inner thighs and the white flesh above the band of her stocking top. She knew exactly what got him hot and how to turn him on. Kid's concentration snapped back when the old man let slip how he could also get his hands on some much stronger material, things of a *specialist nature*.

"It's pretty hardcore stuff mind, not my cup of tea. Some of it's pretty morbid. Torture films, snuff flicks."

Kid's ears pricked up. "I didn't think there was anything such thing as snuff films. I thought it was just the title of a crappy, old Slasher movie."

"Oh no, this stuff's real believe me" Geoff assured him, and then offered to give him the number of a contact in London.

Sue's wild, raunchy antics continued as she got up to fix another round of drinks. The saucy way she carried herself, she just breathed sex. She was forever touching her hair and stroking herself. The way she would walk, or more accurately strut, around the room, displaying her charms, her cleavage thrust out, her ass wiggling, her titties jiggling, the whole brassy works. Sue drove him wild and she knew it, she revelled in it. Kid relished the faint rustle as her killer body rubbed against the flimsy material of her clothing, the subtle swish her nylons made as she crossed and uncrossed her legs. Reading the longing in their faces and keen to push the proceedings along, Geoff upped the ante. Turning to his sexpot wife, he took the flaps of cloth hanging either side of the slit in her skirt, and tore it up the seam, exposing the whole meaty expanse of her left thigh.

"Which side do you prefer now, Kid?" Geoff leered. Sue giggled, swivelling her hips, flaunting both sides of her flanks for his evaluation.

Soon afterwards they retired upstairs to the bedroom, taking their drinks with them. The wood panelled walls, four poster bed and mood lighting lent the room a sexy, Hammer horror ambience. Geoff was one of those garden shed inventors who can turn their clever hands to anything technical, and Kid was made aware that he had the whole room rigged with cameras. He could picture him downstairs in his backroom editing suite, picking his shots from the various camera angles.

Itching for the fuck fest to begin, Kid couldn't wait to get his hands on Sue. He felt like a kid in a candy store. He didn't know what to grab first. Aching with lust, they attacked each other, thrusting their tongues hard down each other's throat until Kid released, pulled back, and licked his tongue across Sue's pursed mouth. He then pushed her off.

"I'm gonna enjoy this," he mused, eyes glinting.

Being a sensualist, the act of unwrapping a woman was

a major part of Kid's thrill, so first he unzipped Sue's skirt, then he ran his hands down her beautiful, bounteous body, savouring how her swollen globes felt through the soft, smooth material. They kissed again, hard. Kid squeezing her fleshy ass, slipping his fingers through her flimsy, lace panties, sliding them down her moist slit. He broke away again and stripped Sue of her top, revealing her black, see-through, décolletage teddy underneath. The sexy outfit emphasising every curve of her hourglass figure. Kneading her mammoth mammaries through the rougher, lacy lingerie, he buried his face in the valley of cleavage.

"I feel like I've died and gone to cleavage heaven," Kid drooled.

He then steered Sue towards the bedroom door and stood her up against it. Once he stripped off his shirt, Kid produced a sleeping mask from the back pocket of his jeans and blindfolded her with it. He then took a set of handcuffs out of his front pocket and clapped them on her wrists.

"Put your arms in the air," Kid commanded brusquely.

As Sue did, he lifted the chain of the cuffs over the brass coat hook on the door, forcing her to totter on her high heels to reach it. Kid gazed at her awhile and drunk it all in. It was a gorgeous sight. Her arms outstretched and rendered above her head, her oxters exposed, her gargantuan tits straining at the seams of her camisole, it all brought a swelling lump to his loins. He felt ravenous. Peeling the straps off her shoulders, Kid unleashed her huge, heaving, pendulous jugs from their confines. They hung heavy, but were firm and stout, without a hint of sag. Despite Sue's age, they'd kept their gelatinous mass. Kid set upon them, smothering his face in her sumptuous cleavage, cupping each hefty breast in both hands as he hunkered down hard on the nipples, sucking on them until they were as hard as bullets. He lifted and squeezed her boobs together, wiping his tongue around her large, brown areolas and licking her erect teats.

Kid then dropped to his knees and ran his hands down the back of her stocking thighs. He loved the sensuous feel of the nylon slipping through his fingers. He hated those bullshit Hollywood movies where the man, or woman, peels her stockings off before they make love. Kid made sure Sue kept her stockings on throughout. As he rubbed his hand between her legs he could feel how wet and turned on she was through the material. Kid snapped the poppers at the crutch and delivered a big, wet, dog lick to her pussy. She tasted fresh and was clean shaven, smooth as a runway. This was a concession on Sue's part. She knew Kid was put off by the unsightly appearance of pubic hair. To him the wiry tangle of a pubic beard looked dingy and unhygienic and seemed too manly on a woman, whereas a cleanshaven snatch felt fresher and looked more feminine and inviting. Kid splayed the lips of her cunt with his fingers and Sue squealed with delight as he clit fucked her with his tongue. She moaned and writhed, rolling her head from side to side on the door, her pelvis undulating as he whisked her off with his middle finger and lapped at her. Kid kept it going until he felt her legs quivering and buckling.

"I want your cock inside me," Sue sighed breathily.

Kid had previously gleaned that, in common with other women her age, Sue preferred penetration to clitoral stimulation. Actually, she couldn't get off properly without it. So even though he got back on his feet, and slipped out of his jeans and Calvin's, he planned to hold out a little longer. He wanted to wait and turn the tables on Sue. Tease *her,* until *she* was begging for it.

As soon as Kid lifted the chain of the handcuffs off the hook, Sue lurched forward uneasy on her feet, and stumbled over to the bed. Still cuffed, she clambered aboard on all fours, her face squashed and crumpled into the mattress, her cunt in the air. Kid kept her in that position by pouncing on her before she could settle. Burying his face in her ass, he spread her cheeks apart and administered one mother of an ass eating. Lingering his tongue back and forth across her asshole, he licked down her crack, dropping to put whole folds of her pussy into his mouth. Sucking and slurping on the tumescent lips, stretching the skin as he pulled back with it still in his mouth, releasing it with a loud juicy smack.

"Oh that feels soooo good," Sue moaned.

Kid could feel the heat from her hot cunt on his face and, once he finished eating her out, he stuffed two forefingers into her wet pussy and worked a thumb in her ass, clutching her in a bowling ball grip. Rubbing them together, he could feel his thumb and fingertips through the thin wall of flesh that separated them. Kid retracted his thumb but carried on fingering her, making a come-hither motion on the spongy lining as he stroked her G-spot. They were so into each other that the room seemed to shrink down and blur out of focus around them, the walls dissolving and melting away as they entered their own sexual realm. Because of this, they rarely noticed Geoff hovering about in the shadows with a hand held camera.

Without speaking, Kid whipped the blindfold off and released the handcuffs. They then maneuvered themselves into a '69' position. With Sue still on all fours, Kid threaded his legs through the arch of her thighs and she lifted her lolling lungs to accommodate him. With eager anticipation, Kid relished that heavenly moment as Sue's mouth closed down to suck on him. She was a world class cocksucker, a virtuoso, slavering all over it like a glutton, licking and kissing the shaft from the root to the tip, without a trace of teeth. Her suction got so hard it felt like she was trying to suck the spunk right out of his body. And the harder she sucked, the further Kid's tongue sank into her gash.

"Oh, come on baby fuck me, I can't take it anymore," Sue gasped.

Neither could he, and with that Kid got up on his knees and

took her from behind, sliding his cock into her hot, succulent slot. As he slid it in Sue let out a deep seated "ooooooh." Sluggish at first, Kid began a gloriously slow fuck, building up his thrusts until he was soon slamming her doggy style. He pounded and pummelled into her, rippling the flesh on her rump. Sue responded with a chorus of high-pitched staccato "uh huh uh huhs," which sounded a bit strange and funny coming from a woman her age.

They're all little girls once they've got a dick inside 'em, Kid sniggered to himself.

When Sue's hand reached back to hold onto his hip Kid swatted it away, and instead he reached his left hand forward and let her suck on his index finger, which hung like a hook out of the corner of her mouth. Kid grabbed the back of her hair with his other hand and squeezed it into a tight fist. Sue's head craned back as he pulled on it, creating a curve in her spine. From a side view he could see her ten gallon jugs swinging like udders, rocking back and forth as he banged the shit out of her. It was a beautiful sight and, just as before, Kid was impressed by the vigour of her body.

As they fucked, Kid could see the pained and twisted expressions of sexual pleasure on Sue's face reflected in the cheval mirror that stood by the bed. He loved watching the gritted teeth aggression, her face all scrunched up, curling her top lip or biting her bottom one. These out of control expressions took Kid over the brink and, as Sue spasmed, he pulled out and wrenched a hot, arcing, torrent of spunk across her back, cackling aloud once he came.

Women weren't the only ones who could enjoy multiple orgasms. When Kid was this turned on he could cum six or seven times without losing a hard-on. This ability was one of the reasons why Sue offered him the gig.

The action cuts to a TV monitor downstairs broadcasting the footage from the bedroom. Using some of his spilt semen as lubrication, Kid stirs the slop in her asshole with his cock, and slowly plunges it in. The back door entry draws a throaty groan out from Sue lungs, and she's soon seething through gritted teeth as he reams her out.

"This'll put a wiggle in your walk," Kid wisecracks, spanking her hard on her lofted rump.

JUMP CUT: Sue's now on her back with her legs hiked up as Kid repeatedly slams into her.

"Fuck me into the wall," she pleads, her titties splayed and spinning like plates as she gazes down between her legs, watching intently as his cock rams into her. Kid spritzes then whips her pussy with his dick, rubbing it against her clit.

They switch positions and Sue gets on top. She lets out a deep seated "ahhhh," as she impales herself and slides down Kid's shaft. She makes a gyrating motion, like a mother hen settling on her eggs, as she accommodates him, and smiles to herself contentedly, her eyes closed. She then starts riding him. She bucks, rockin' n rollin' her cunt around, grinding her pussy down hard on his pelvic bone, scratching her clit against his pubic hair. She writhes and squeezes those big old titties together, tweaking her nipples, her eyes squinting, her nostrils flaring, her head tilted back in ecstasy. When she cums, she flexes the muscles in the neck of her cunt, clamping his cock in a vise-like grip. She releases it and dismounts, giggling while Kid pleads for the friction of fucking to begin again.

JUMP CUT: Acting on Kid's instructions, Sue lays on her right side with her left knee bent into her stomach. Kid straddles her prone leg and slots into a position that offers the deepest penetration. Kid can feel his cock hitting her cervix.

"I LOVE fucking you," he enthuses.

"God, I can feel it in my throat," Sue pants.

"Flatterer," Kid beams.

The action switches back to bedroom. Kid picks up an empty beer bottle from the bedside table and waves it in the air, the wedge of desiccated lime rattles inside it. Sue is lying on her back with her legs apart. Parting the lips of her cunt with his left hand, Kid inserts the neck of the bottle inside her, twirling it as he eases it in, until it is squashed up against her lips. With an eye on the camera, Kid leaves the bottle half hanging out for a moment for a nice visual and then proceeds to fuck her with it. Come morning the bottle is caked in a dry, white cloudy slime, and a close up of it is used as the final shot of this homemade porno.

CUT BACK: Video footage on the TV monitor. Sue is posed completely naked, her bare back to camera. Her leg raised, she rests a stiletto heel on the foot of the bed. A close up captures the sheen of her legs. Kid is slumped beneath her, his head obscured and buried between her legs. Sue's plump, pillowy caboose juts out and gyrates as Kid suckles her cunt. His face emerges and he licks along the flank of her thigh, running his tongue down the back of her calf to the ankle chain above the ridge of her heel.

JUMP CUT: Pumping his joint in his fist, Kid ejaculates all over the anklet, his milky semen dribbling down Sue's foot towards the tip of her stiletto. Sue sits on the edge of the bed and removes the high-heel. Cupping the icky foot in both hands, she lifts it like a communion dish to her lips and laps the spermy sacrament off.

CUT BACK: The bedroom. Sue is on her back and Kid is on top in a reverse '69'. Sue flips Kid's cock back between his legs and milks him into her mouth. She then returns the ass eating compliment and Kid can, somehow, feel the scales on the surface of her tongue as she does. The tonguing sends a bolt of blood surging through his cock and, as they go at it again, a purposeful close up of Sue's fingers, shows her wedding band smothered in cum.

JUMP BACK: Video footage. So as not to obscure his view or distract her from all her good work, Kid gathers Sue's hair up into a bunch as she sucks him off. He marvels at the zealous way she devours it, breathing heavily as she slavishly blows him, which not only underlines her pleasure, but also adds to his own. Sue stops sucking his cock for a moment and plays with it. Resting the tip between her nose and top lip, she kisses it then rolls it across her face, slapping his cock against her cheeks and brushing it across her pouting lips.

JUMP CUT: Sex is never hotter than when there's a hint of hostility and they both loved it rough. Kid grips a fat ample tit in one hand and slaps it hard with the other. Sue giggles as he bats them around, then shimmies her shoulders, jiggling them in front of him. Cupping her tits together, she lifts and offers them up to him and Kid jerks off and cums all over her cleavage. Sue massages the semen into her skin and the bleachy aroma fumes off her chest, filling their nostrils.

CUT BACK: Bedroom. Kid is cracking Sue up doing a camp impression of Sharon Stone in *Basic Instinct*. Resting against the headboard with a cigarette in hand, Kid rubs one leg up and down the other and purrs, "Have you ever fucked on cocaine baby? It's nice." Sue chuckles, standing totally starkers at the foot of the bed, hands on hips. Her four inch heels kick her ass up in the air, so she tilts forward slightly as she totters about. Kid appraises her wafted hindquarters. "Hell of a wagon ya draggin," he leers.

CUT BACK: Video. Lying on her back Sue squeezes her breasts together while Kid straddles and tit fucks her. With her mouth agape and her chin buried in her chest, Sue sucks the head of his cock as he thrusts between those beauties. All of a sudden, Kid springs off the mattress and splatters his spunk across the cheval mirror next to the bed. Mindful of the movie being made of all this, Sue hops off the bed, kneels, and licks the cum off the glass, moping it up with whorish relish.

Downstairs later, Kid enjoyed a post-coital tequila and joint in the living room. With Geoff busy editing a rough copy of the tape together, and Sue upstairs taking a shower, he chilled out and relaxed, listening to the Nat King Cole LP he'd put on. It seemed the perfect touch. Draping his legs over the arm of the chair, Kid sparked a match on the zipper of his fly and fired up the joint. He kicked back and listened to that beautiful, velvety voice crooning the mystical *Nature Boy*, digging his high, feeling buzzed, sleepy and spent.

"There was a boy, a very strange enchanted boy......"

Kid struggled to keep his eyes open as he fought the heavy tugs of sleep bearing down on him. It felt like the full force of gravity itself was pressing his head back hard into the cushions. Thoughts just floated away, like a train shoving off from a platform with a soft sudden jolt.

Kid finds himself whizzing round the streets of LA on a motorised bed, checking out the Beverly Hills homes of the rich and famous. He's on the verge of spinning out of control but, as he takes a bend, he just manages to right the vehicle. Looking for action, he cruises down Sunset Strip. En route, he's overtaken by three unsavoury-looking bikers. One of the riders seems to have second thoughts and pulls back, drawing up alongside him. As they cruise along, the biker does a crafty Q&A with him and Kid senses something's afoot. Although part of him is excited to talk to a real life Hells Angel, Kid's gut instinct tells him it's all a ruse and the bikers are using the conversation to gauge his accent and nationality. The biker asks if Kid knows such and such a place in London. Kid is polite and goes along with it, even though he knows the biker is just stringing him along, having already sussed he's a tourist. The two other bikers join them. Kid pulls ahead and tries to get away from them, but overhears one say, "He'll have money and a passport on him." Kid's heart sinks as they overtake and force him to pull over onto the hard shoulder. Before Kid can escape he's apprehended and frogmarched off to a motorway underpass.

Kid knows he's in serious trouble and a pit opens in his stomach. Panic stricken, he calls out to a lovely looking latina, selling beverages in her roadside cantina, but she just smiles back and winks at the head biker. Thankfully a police car pulls up and two cops get out, but Kid's relief is short lived as they just fall in and follow. Finally, Kid cries for help to a kindly looking, old, black man running a market stall, selling batteries, lighters and such, but he just moves out from behind his table and joins them in the shadows beneath the flyover. They all crowd around as the bikers pat Kid down and fleece him of his money and ID. Kid is then forced onto his knees and his hands are tied behind his back. The cops, bikers and black guy start unzipping. It turns out they're all part of a rob and rape crew that preys on unsuspecting travellers.

Before the wicked deed can be done, Kid finds himself in the bowels of a building. It has an antiseptic atmosphere, and the gloomy decor, polished floors and emergency swing doors suggest it's the basement of a New York hospital. A black kid comes crashing through the swing doors to Kid's right, propelled into the corridor by unseen hands. He wheels around like a drunken cowboy ejected from a saloon and, dazed and confused, staggers onwards, lurching through the opaque, plastic curtains that drape the entrance of what appears to be a morgue-cum-slaughterhouse. As the youth tumbles through the flaps, Kid's eyes pan up to read the sign above the entrance: THE VIPER ROOM. The acronym stands for *Violent Interrogations, Punishments and Execution Rituals.*

A terrible evil radiates from the room, and Kid can just imagine the horrors that await the young man inside. The tortures made all the more worse by the realisation that no one will be able to hear his agonised screams all the way down here. Creeped out, Kid turns and takes off down the corridor, heading for the fire exit at the end. However, as he runs the corridor distends, lengthening out before him. The fire exit receding into the distance, so the more he runs the further away it becomes. It's like he's running on the spot. His legs are like lead weights, unable to make any progress. Fearing pursuit, Kid hits full pelt and gradually makes up ground as the corridor ceases to elongate. But when he reaches the fire exit he's dismayed to find he can't open the door. Again, fear gives him strength and, putting his full weight behind it, he hits the push bar and busts his way through, only to discover another closed door behind it. This door opens easily, however, and he enters a darkened room. The place feels haunted, and as he crosses the threshold a ghostly voice whispers, "ZOOM." Floating above him, just beneath the bare, blinking light bulb hanging from the ceiling, he finds a collection of copper coins spinning slowly in the air.

The action cuts to a ranch somewhere in Tornado Alley. From the seclusion of a porch window, Kid watches a twister spiralling across the prairie. As it moves closer, the sun catches the glint of a chrome, hexagonal shaped UFO caught up in its whirl. The tornado seems to be heading directly for the ranch, so Kid races to a tumbledown barn and takes refuge in the hayloft, waiting for the windstorm to pass over....

A FLASH IMAGE: Back in the basement of the hospital, a trio of strange looking fetuses fly down the long, dark corridor, trailing their umbilical cords like balloons on string.

It feels like an earthquake hits the barn as the cyclone rips the roof off and Kid finds the UFO hovering directly above him. A liquid crystal display screen on the undercarriage projects a live video image of himself looking up at the craft. The sound of footsteps ushers the presence of somebody scuffling up the last few wooden steps to the hayloft. A visitor, beamed down from the craft, emerges in profile, looking straight ahead. Only as he reaches the top of the stairs does his head turn towards him in robotic, slow motion. He faces Kid head on. The visitor looks like the quintessential mad scientist with big, bulging, googly eyes, a maniacal expression, and tufts of hair sticking up either side of his bald dome. Like an assassin guided by remote control, he advances, coming for him.......

"WHERE DO THEY COME FROM? WHERE DO THEY GO?"

With those nagging words reverberating in his head, Kid awoke with a start, just as Sue entered the room. He was surprised to find her covered head to toe in a long, black hooded robe and cradling a child in her arms. It was coddled up in a tight blanket. Sue brought the bundle over to him, proffering it for his inspection. But as Kid arose from the chair, he instinctively sensed something was amiss. He peered in gingerly, then flinched back with alarm, freaked out by the queer, unearthly visage gazing back at him. It was creepy looking and ghoulish. Its piggy eyes, blighted by what appeared to be cataracts, were set in the deep recesses of an outsized skull, shaped like an upside-down pear. It had jaundice-coloured skin and a pinched and puckered face that seemed to have been pieced together like an identikit picture. Built up, using the facial characteristics of a hobgoblin and a witchy old crone, a hooked nose, pointy ears and a bony chin, its spooky, withered features appeared both aged and infant and its aura, too, conveyed the same sense of helplessness and fragility that marks both the frail and the newborn.

Cooing perversely, Sue fawned over the unsightly, little freak.

"How's my little piglet then? How's my little poppet?"

Kid frowned at her incredulously, repulsed by her screwy dotage.

"Is it yours? What is it?"

As soon as he asked the question, an answer of sorts came back at him as he heard the word "sentinel" spoken inside his head. Kid knew Sue hadn't said anything, it was as though the word had been planted there.

"Where did it come from?" Kid asked.

"You could call it manna from heaven," Sue replied cryptically, grinning to herself. She then proceeded to unravel the blanket.

"Take a look at this."

The blanket opened to reveal the bony chest and navel and the creatures distended stomach. It seemed to be made out of a hollow, see-through, fiberglass material as a glowing amber light shone through it. The creature was lit from within.

"The colours change depending on his moods," Sue explained and, as if on cue, the alien child ran through it's kaleidoscope of colours. There was a rainbow of emotions, beginning with amber, denoting peace and contentment, altering, dramatically, to an indigo blue that transmitted grief, sorrow and anxiety. Darkening further to a black, purplish hue, conveying depression and out and out despair. The belly then flared up red, radiating hate, anger, and passion, lightening to yellow, the colour of trauma. Gold seemed to signify love, while silver denoted serenity and enlightenment. The demonstration ended with a dark bottle green, indicating melancholy and nostalgia.

"The green, the green, the green, the green," the curio trilled in high key distress. The outburst made Kid jump. The creature's voice was metallic and distorted and each word, though intelligible, sounded like a fork being scraped across a dinner plate. The voice cut straight through him and put his teeth on edge. The words seemed to come in waves, passing through the creature as if beamed down from a remote location.

"He speaks very advanced for his age," Sue beamed with inane, motherly pride. But her human/alien offspring quickly became irritable, wriggling in her arms, whining petulantly, "You hurted me mummy, you hurted me."

As the child struggled, the blanket loosened and fell away and Kid discovered its arms were made out of sticky, luminous green slime, the kind you find in a novelty shop. Despite Sue's attempts to placate and pacify the child, the squinnying continued and the whiny, babyish voice was so nauseating it triggered a deep, sadistic impulse in him. This baneful compulsion made Kid's teeth grit and his stomach tighten, and his body became weak and momentarily debilitated. A panging ache sizzled across the backs of his legs as he thought of bashing the baby's brains in. An image of a lion attacking a rival's cubs when it takes over a new pride flashed through Kid's head. He resisted the temptation and snatched the space oddity out of Sue's arms instead, throwing it across the room. It landed behind the sofa, but, strangely, rather than hearing a dull thump at the moment of impact, it emitted a high-pitched squeak, as if it were a toy.

"Ouch.... you poo pooed me," the creature bleated in a little lost voice and then....... nothing.

A tense, pregnant pause fell over the room. Kid and Sue looked at each other and then gazed over, expectantly, in the direction of where the creature lay unseen. Hearing no sound, they creeped towards the sofa, cautiously, hesitating for a moment, before peeking behind the back of the couch. Their screams shattered the uneasy silence as they jumped out of their skins, startled by the alien child who whizzed past their faces as it sprung back to life. The creature pinged around the room, ricocheting like a rubber ball. Rebounding off the ceiling and walls, knocking down pictures and plaques, its body all a blur like a souped-up cartoon character. Finally, it bounced back into its mother's arms and came to rest. However, following its whirlwind exertions, its sticky, green arms had gotten all tangled up around its body, leaving it straight jacketed in its own slime.

CHAPTER 6
TABETH ALI

Astral Boy's jaunt in New York was really working out. To begin with, the interview with Ice-T went swimmingly. Things got off to a good start when he presented the rapper with a few recent copies of*Hustler*, and once they started discussing their favourite porn stars they never looked back. In return, he ended up with a backstage pass to the Bodycount gig where, at Ice's insistence, he watched the entire show from the side of the stage.

His experiences at the Research Center proved fruitful too. Under hypnosis, the professor put him through a series of tests designed to build up his mental stamina and galvanise his powers of visualization. By the end of it, he was able to actualise a mocked-up facsimile of his own body and use it as a vehicle to project himself out into the world, without any physical restrictions. It was mentally exhausting, but with practice he would soon be able to travel around for hours at will.

His first proper attempt at remote viewing went well, even if the final part was obviously inspired by the recent, big interview he did. Professor Litvinov reads a transcript of what Astral Boy saw in his study, "I'm in LA, up at the Griffith Park Observatory, looking through one of the telescopes, scanning the streets below. I focus on a black cop standing by his patrol car down on Sunset Strip. The cop points to a funnel of black smoke billowing up into the chlorine blue sky. You can just make out the sound of the riots flaring up downtown. It's like the far off roar you hear when you pass a football stadium and a goal is scored.

"Launched down an aluminium chute, I land with a jump onto a graffiti covered stage, littered with debris. Broken pipes, shards of glass and pieces of drift wood. Looking around, I discover the stage is actually the floor of stationary boxcar, its sliding doors open on both sides. Without warning, this relic from an old western movie becomes engulfed in a passing tornado and, for no good reason, I pick up an iron bar and hurl it out into the void, where it's immediately caught up in the whirlwind. Holding onto the door frame for dear life, I gingerly peek outside and just manage to pull my head back in time as the bar *whooshes* past my face. Searching for a way out, I discover a trap door in the floor. I open it, and climb down a ladder until I find myself on the edge of a swimming pool in a subterranean grotto. Twinkling lights reflect off the surface of the water, and dance across the walls and rock barrelled ceiling. The bleachy aroma of chlorine never fails to stir that stomach churning dread I used to feel as a boy, riding the school bus to the swimming baths, agonising throughout the journey because I couldn't swim and was terrified of the water. I leave through a side door and end up wandering down a series of tunnels, illuminated by oil lamps. Trying to find a way out, I follow some rusting, disused monorail tracks, figuring they must eventually lead out to an exit. En route, I find a discarded magazine half buried in the dirt: *CADAVERS*. The front cover depicts a voluptuous slave girl in PVC bondage gear being hoisted up on a pulley, her hands tied high above her head exposing her oxters. The slave demurs under the abusive thrall of a striking, whip wielding dominatrix, her hot body squeezing out of a rubber cat suit. Her flawless features brought out by a black latex skullcap covering her neck, scalp and forehead, lets her long, flaxen mane spilling out from the hole in the crown. I flick through the pages. The contents include an all too graphic series of death scenes culled from the LAPD police files of the 1930s and 40s. Bodies mangled in car wrecks, suicides caught on camera, and Weegee's famous, on the spot snapshots of murder and violence. There was a ghoulish pictorial on the Guanajuato Mummies of Mexico, and an article on the Nazi expeditions into Nepal that included photographs of a Tibetan sky burial. Because the ground was too rocky to dig there, and trees were too scarce to use for cremations, corpses were laid out on a large, flat stone instead. There, the skin is flayed, the limbs hacked off, and the bones bashed to dust with rocks, the meat cut up into small pieces and left on a mountaintop for the vultures to consume or carry away.

"Under the headline, *Monroe Cost Us A Million*, a Fortean news story disclosed how a specially formulated anti-aging cream, exclusively concocted for, and used by, the late screen goddess Marilyn Monroe, could have, in this day and age, been used to save the lives of an estimated one million people. However, such was her insatiable demand for the ointment, the Hollywood legend used up every last drop, leaving the secret ingredients of the miraculous compound a mystery for decades. Set against the article was the last image ever taken of the sad, tragic icon, a headshot of her in repose, laid out on the mortuary slab. As the discolouration of her skin pigment has already set in, she appears semi-simian.

"I trek on, and finally come to an opening in the side of a hill, and it feels great to breathe fresh air again. Digging my heels in, I skid down a slag heap to the condemned grounds of what was once the Los Angeles Zoo. The sprawling menagerie is now the home and habitat of mutants, human abominations and other aborted freaks. From a safe distance overlooking the rock garden, I spy a pride of slumbering Astral dogs, lounging on a stone plateau, carved from a colossal, hollowed out boulder. The hulking, rock stone resembles a toothless mouth. The lower lip providing a porch for the dogs to bask in the sun, while the overhanging upper lip acts as an awning, and gives shelter from the rain on stormy afternoons like this. I gaze on in amazement as a double-headed doberman shows up. It's joined at the midriff, so each head takes turns to sniff the ground for terrestrial scents. A pair of phantom dogs then appear in the guise of two ink-black stingrays. They skim over the terrain, scampering with tentacles for legs and pectoral fins flapping like bat wings. Vaulting onto a rock, they shape-shift in midair into doe-eyed mongrels and land shivering and baring their teeth in a hideous grimace, a reaction brought on by their physiological alteration.

"Rustling out from the brush, a deformed feral boy breaks cover. He's paralysed from the waist down, so he's forced to drag his lower limbs around like a dead weight, using just his hands and elbows. Wriggling on his belly, the savage inches up the side of the boulder and, with laborious effort, worms his way onto the plateau. With slug-like deliberation he crawls over to an Astral dog busy noshing on a scrap of raw meat. The boy raps his knuckle hard on the animal's nose and it yelps and scurries away, leaving him to polish off the revolting remnants of the semi-masticated meal.

Zoning

"That night, I go flying with Ice-T in his personal helicopter, the craft wheeling over the glittering cityscape below. At one point a police chopper draws up alongside."

"Christ, man, they even sweat you up here?"

"Piloting, Ice nonchalantly looks past me and surveys the 'ghetto bird' with a cool disfavour, 'Nah, man, the pigs don't give me no static up here.'

"The police chopper keeps up with us for a while, just enough time to run a license check, and then it banks off to the right.

"Giant klieg lights crisscross the night sky. The atmosphere is warm and enclosed as if the city is ceilinged. Ice dips the chopper low and we zoom between buildings, skimming above the streets and the ratty looking palm trees. As I fix my eyes and concentrate hard on what I'm seeing, I realise that what I had presumed was the LA basin is, in reality, not a city at all, but a miniature model set consisting of skyscrapers shaped from stickle brick blocks and the heads of Remington shavers. Office buildings have been built from electrical transformers, while apartment complexes are just cardboard boxes, painted and lit up inside so the rooms look occupied through the windows. A warehouse district is made up entirely of flight cases, and I can now see that the boulevards and avenues are actually the grooves and grid of a gigantic, electrical circuit board, masquerading as a sprawling conurbation. The whole optical illusion created on a vast sound stage for a Hollywood movie."

The sound of Blondie's *Atomic* blasts from a cranked-up stereo through an open bedroom window in Stratford House, and rings out over the Somerstown Estates. Skyrise Kid moseys along the ground floor walkway of Oldbury House, savouring the mouthwatering aroma of roast dinners wafting through the window of each kitchen he passes, each Sunday dinner with its own individual flavour.

He slams through the stairwell doors and joins the other elder Skyrise Muthas sitting smoking on the benches on the concourse. They watch as the younger kids play a game of *Kick Ball Trot*. The game was basically an extension of hide and seek, but using a stationary football as the base. You could either tap your foot and get *in*, so long as you could get there ahead of whoever was doing the seeking, or if some kids had already been caught, you could kick the football away and release them, leaving whoever was *it* to traipse off sluggishly, retrieve the ball, and put it back on its spot, giving the others time to scarper off and hide again.

Kid leaves the group and sits on the guardrail girding the grassland of Longbridge House. Bored, he idly picks at the chipped white paint, exposing the iron underneath, wincing when a piece lodges painfully under his fingernail. As he lights a cigarette a young, nubile woman emerges from the corridor of the Longbridge stairwell pushing a buggy. He recognized her from school. Annette was the cousin of his best mate, and although a couple of years below him, they'd always been friendly, and he knew all about the schoolgirl crush she reportedly had on him. Even though Kid fancied her he did nothing about it at the time because of her age. Now here she was, five years later, all grown up and already a teenaged mum. She looked hot, mind you. She had blossomed into a right little thruster, her titties bursting out of her low cut top, and her bubble butt squeezed into a tight pair of *Daisy Duke* denim cut offs worn over black tights and boots. The sexy get up showed her juicy body off and Kid was turned on from the jump. He couldn't wait to get his hands on her. Figuring she must have been visiting a local friend, as he knew she didn't live on any of the estates, Kid was somewhat surprised when some of the Skyrise Muthas began bantering with her in an overly familiar manner.

"Oi, look, here comes another one, dropped a sprog just to get a council flat on the social," mocked Bomber Essery, a suedeheaded youth with an unfortunate port-wine stain covering the left side of his face.

"Yeah, keep taking the tablets baby," Bronx sniggered with a cheeky grin.

Annette smiled meekly at their sarky jibes and carried on walking. Kid didn't get the last quip until his cousin Gemma, who was in the same year at school with Annette and knew her a little, confided, "I heard she's gone a bit dinny in the head."

"Yeah, the wheels go round but the hamster's dead," Bronx wisecracked, twirling his forefinger at the side of his head.

While the others left it at that, Kid took off after Annette, who wandered off up the pedestrian walkway, heading in the direction of Skyrise Block. Walking with her head down, she hadn't noticed him as she passed by. So when Kid caught up her he tapped her on the shoulder, delivering a, "D'ya remember me?" Turning round he was taken aback by just how downcast and withdrawn the girl was. "So you're on the *Mogadon* are ya?" Kid teased, trying to raise a smile. Grinning through her gloom, Annette replied ruefully, "I keep getting pregnant, but now I'm just starting to have boys." That was a bit of a weird thing to say, but Kid brushed it aside, crouched, and feigned an interest in her newest born. It turned out she *was* on her way to see a friend, but wasn't much looking forward to it, so instead they decided to catch up on old times, and find out what had happened to some of the people they knew from school. Kid lifted the buggy over the guard rail and they sat on the grass shooting the breeze.

Annette's olive skin, dark hair and brown eyes was down to her Maltese roots. She was certainly comely and curvaceous, but there was a vague haziness about her now, that was never there before, a slow reacting, somnambulant quality as if she was sleepwalking through life. This, combined with her husky voice, suggested, at best, a sleepy, smouldering sexuality, and at worst, someone who was a little bit backwards.

As they chatted, it became obvious there was an instant sexual attraction between them. Kid could tell from the lingering looks. As they read the yearning in each other's eyes, there was a subliminal recognition and acceptance of where things were going. Kid planted the thought in her mind and watched it flower in her face. He didn't know her domestic situation, but as they began kissing he could tell she hadn't been shown much tenderness and affection in a while by the way her lips fumbled against his. She probably wasn't used to a guy taking his time and kissing her properly and, as a result, she was slow to catch on at first. However, she soon picked up and, in no time at all, she was eagerly responding, thrusting her tongue passionately into his mouth.

Kid's stomach fluttered as a slither of sexual excitement snaked across it, and he couldn't resist grabbing a handful of tit. Braless, the teats of her budding breasts peeked through the soft, smooth material.

Aware they were in plain view of people, they decided to repair to the relative seclusion of the Halesowen stairwell. Fortuitously, the windows of the stairwell had been smashed in and boarded up with plywood, perfect for keeping out the prying eyes of passersby. Kid wedged the buggy against the inside of the stairwell door, so that the child was facing away from them. They then tore at each other's clothes, sucking hard on one other's tongues. Dropping to his knees he unbuttoned Annette's shorts and ripped a hole in the crotch of her tights. Her pussy was shaved at the sides into a wispy quiff. Ravenously, he began eating her out, Kid tasting that familiar, sour grapefruit tang of cunt. Splaying her moist lips, he darted his tongue all over her clit, flicking it in and out of her hole. Annette's pelvis gyrated, and he could feel her legs buckle and tremble as he licked her out. Their insides fluttering with the sex ache, Kid rose to his feet and pressed her hard up against the wall. He unzipped his jeans and sprung his cock.

Zoning

"I'm gonna fuck you sooo good," Kid whispered in her ear, and lifting her right leg, he slid his hard as steel cock into her wet, sopping mush. Annette released a loud, deep seated moan as it sunk in. As he raucously piston pumped her, Kid kept a haphazard look out for anybody approaching. The window of the stairwell door on his right opened on to the ground floor landing of Halesowen House, and it gave him a clear view of the front courts and most of the car park.

As he plowed away rampantly, Kid pawed Annette's tits, gnawing on her battered, baby-suckled nipples, like chewed up cherries. The dark freckles peppered across her cleavage drove him wild, as did her square jaw-line and insolent mouth, reminiscent of a young Jane Russell. Mindful of their surroundings, Kid put his hand over Annette's mouth to muffle her histrionics. But their carnal revelry was broken, for a moment anyway, by the siren wail of a cop car cruising nearby. An audible threat that not only heightened their headlong thrill and accelerated Kid's frenzied strokes, but also renewed the risk of them being caught fucking *in flagrante*.

Thankfully the siren died, and as they fucked on Kid watched the twisted and contorted expressions breaking across Annette's face, that pornographic look of pleasure and pain. He banged her senseless, and felt her body spasm and tremble, quivering as she convulsed and began to orgasm. The last thing this poor cow needed was another kid, so when he felt his own legs buckle, Kid pulled out and started wanking furiously before her. Taking his cue, Annette slid down the wall and squatted before him, her tongue hanging out of her wide, outstretched mouth. Kid shot thick globules of spunk down her throat and across her upturned face, christening her forehead. Then grasping her jaw in his left hand, Kid slapped his cock against that insolent mouth, wiping his shaft across her lips, his cum dribbling down her chin. He made sure to clean her up before they left, and as they pulled their clothes together, Annette kissed Kid's chest, flushed with a hot, blotchy sex rash.

Departing the stairwell, blushing and rubber-legged, they found a throng of local residents in front of Skyrise Block, rubbernecking a crime scene. Police were busy cordoning off the area around the Longbridge stairwell with yellow tape. The crime scene consisted of an abandoned 1955 Chevy which had been parked up on the pavement by the rose garden. On the bonnet were what appeared to be skeletal remains, ritually arranged to form some kind of symbol, like characters from Chinese writing. Long, humerus bones crisscrossed each other at the foot of one symbol, while smaller fibula bones formed a lantern shape above another. Lying next to the car was the corpse of an Astral dog, its flanks and ribs punctured with skewers to prop it up on its back, so that its legs stuck up in the air. Moving in for a closer look, Annette and Kid overheard one of the forensic guys tell a colleague how the dog had been exanguinated, totally drained of blood.

Astral Boy's second attempt at remote viewing was far more successful, because he not only managed to inhabit another person's body, but he was also able to travel back in time to Bronze Age, Mesopotamia...

"I look through the eyes of a neophyte as he descends the stone steps of the amphitheatre. The structure has been built into the cavity of a vast crater, formed when a crystal orb struck the dunes many centuries ago. The blast had melted the sand into glass fulgurite that crunches beneath your feet. The neophyte cuts through the assembled mass of worshippers. They're a bedraggled bunch, dressed in sackcloth robes, with long, matted hair and scraggly beards. They look like beggars. He pushes through the shabby horde and works his way to the front of the stage, ready to pay homage. Above him, an altar is set up on a raised platform.

Once the sun sets, the ceremony begins, and Tabeth Ali takes the stage to a roaring ovation. He is of Persian origin, but has chrome coloured eyes and a wild shock of dreadlocks. With his burnished skin and wizened features he seems both ancient and timeless. He lays his slender, half naked body upon the wooden altar and begins meditating. He is then joined on stage by his well-built Berber assistant, carrying a lit torch. The stone-faced man stands guard over the recumbent body, waiting. The crowd surges forward expectantly. As soon as his master is in a deep trance, the assistant mouths some unintelligible words, and then sets fire to the altar. The flames spark off a spate of suicides and celebratory murders, all carried out as sacrificial offerings to their idol. Engulfed in hoops of blue flames, Tabeth Ali rises slowly from his sleeping position. Though ablaze his body doesn't burn. Instead of disintegrating, his flesh withstands the heat and conducts it like wood. While he's still in trance, his assistant presents him with a pair of golden shears, and taking them in his flaming right hand, he snips off the fingertips on his other hand. The severed stubs fly into the air and rain down in a torrent of blood, baptising the neophyte who's busy testifying below."

Skyrise Kid threads his hang glider between two tower blocks along the seafront. Landing zones run down the entire side of the buildings like a spinal column. They look like out-sized versions of those flashing bumpers you find in pinball machines. Negotiating the wafting thermals, Kid taxis his craft and drops it ten feet, savouring the dipping sensation in his stomach. A scratchy picture, transmitted from a camera fixed at the front of his crash helmet, shows his glider-eye view as he prepares to land. Catching a perfect pocket of air, he gracefully sweeps down onto the landing zone, tiptoeing deftly across its surface. Perched, Kid sets the glider down, and unzips his black canvas jumpsuit. He surveys the vista of the White City seafront spread out before him, a five mile esplanade, stretching from the beaches of Eastney to the left, to the Ferris wheel, dockyard and harbour to the right. A sweeping panorama broken in the middle by South Parade pier, which juts out into the Solent, a stretch of water separating the Isle of Wight from the mainland. From this bird's eye view, he can see the tracks of the monorail that have been laid out over the roofs of all the buildings. You can ride these rails like a roller coaster and travel over the rooftops across the city. Skyrise Kid zips up, casts off and glides down to the ground, hitting the street running.

On a balmy summer's evening, spectators have gathered at the Round Tower overlooking the Solent, a site used historically to wave the fleets out and welcome them back home again. A news reporter, microphone in hand, does a piece to camera for the local TV station. The image cuts to passengers boarding the top deck of an open-top sea taxi, docked at the nearby ferry terminal. As night draws on, a carnival atmosphere sets in and music rings out from ravers partying on shore. A huge cheer goes up as the top deck of the sea craft is set alight and then cast across the harbour like a funeral pyre. In a graphic close-up, the television cameras capture the flames billowing off the passengers' heads as they're burnt alive. The vessel is on a pre-set collision course, and the TV cameras follow its progress, capturing the moment it batters into one of the sea forts, a mile or so out to sea. The explosion lights up the night sky like fireworks, to a crescendo of jubilation from the drunken revellers.

Nearby, the fairground has become a ghost town, and a spectral aroma of hot dog onions and candy floss hangs in the air. Skyrise Muthas have convened at the Hot Walls at the rear exit, where an amusement arcade stands adjacent on a jetty. Taking turns, the boys run along the wall, swinging from a rope hung from a hook in the sky. Executing large, giddy arcs they launch themselves off and dive bomb into the sea, adolescent excitement rolling inside them.

Skyrise Kid hang glides through the night sky. He spies an auto graveyard below, lit by floodlights on each corner of the perimeter fence. In the middle of the yard stands a tire mountain surrounded by burnt out wrecks. A soaring rise goes up in his stomach as he swoops down and settles on the roof of a beaten up 1955 Chevy. He unbuckles himself from his craft and sets it down on the roof, he then jumps onto the bonnet and lays down, resting his back against the windscreen. Drunk, he spreads his arms out in a crucifix pose. Next thing he knows, Kid slides off the hood and takes off, flying by the seat of his pants on a magic carpet. Hovering just inches off the ground, he rides roughshod over nebulous bumps in the road as he hurtles down the night time streets of South London. He travels so fast that his surroundings become a blur, the lights from the grotty shop fronts and streetlamps turning into long, trailing, luminous streamers.

He heads north up Balham High Road, over Balham Hill, cutting through Clapham and Kennington, a clear unbroken run to Waterloo, then across the Thames to Piccadilly and the heart of London. Rushing around the London Underground, the subway system a vast, endless, labyrinthine maze of escalators, platforms and inter-connecting tunnels. Travelling up and down all the levels feels like snakes and ladders.

Kid exits the Trocadero and takes his place in a queue outside a West End theatre on the Soho side of Shaftsbury Avenue. He knows the play stars Alan Bates because his name appears on the marquee. Although the box office cubicle is empty, Kid still slips his ticket through the window, and heaves through the clacking turnstile to enter. He finds himself alone in an empty Moroccan tea room back in Tangier. It's a swanky joint, decorated in the traditional Moorish style, with mosaic tiling and low level tables and seating cushions. The place is shrouded in a late afternoon gloom, the only light coming through the French doors in the middle of the room. Kid exits these doors and walks out through the Piccadilly shopping arcade, the posh display windows of the jewellers and upmarket gentlemens' outfitters on either side of him.

Wandering on, his immediate surroundings begin to synthesize, as a back alley in Tangier morphs into the main drag of White City. This composite milieu merging together like a double exposure created on a photograph. Kid roams along a narrow side street winding down from the medina which leads out to the Petit Socco, or "little square," up ahead. On his right he passes a hole in the wall bazaar chock full of tourist tat: brass ornaments, leather goods, vintage postcards and other antique junk. Coming up on his left he finds a row of British high street shops: a dingy hairdressers, a slot machine arcade, a Circle K newsagent. The remnants of a main road, blasting through the guts of the Spanish hotel situated in the heart of the souk. Kid feels like a crustacean, trailing the cavernous maze of the Kasbah like a shell on his back.

He runs into Ahmed, his gracious Moroccan tourist guide, dressed in a long, cream coloured djellaba and fez, who promptly whisks him back to their hideaway hangout, the Cafe Hafa. In town, the facades of the hashish cafes are adorned with beautifully garish murals displaying cartoonish images of female genies advertising their wares inside, however, the Cafe Hafa was different. An open aired café, set on a cliffside, overlooking the Straits of Gibraltar. You could while away the hours, smoking kif and drinking mint tea, getting high while local patrons played chess, and pussycats nudged about your feet. Tucked away from the tourist traps and off the beaten track, it was a hidden treasure, a real gem.

Hours passed, swapping stories. As they nursed their drinks, Ahmed shared an amusing anecdote about one former customer who got so stoned there he described seeing a housewife darning some socks through the window of her apartment all the way over in *Gibraltar*.

He also told Kid about the time, back in the sixties, when he escorted Brian Jones from the Rolling Stones on his visit here to record the Master Musicians of Joujouka up at their village in the foothills of the Rif Mountains. The rock star had become fascinated with the Sufi musicians' wild, free-form folk music and was interested in incorporating their primeval rhythms into the Stones' sound. This seemed most appropriate for a group whom William S. Burroughs once, memorably, described as a "four thousand year old rock and roll band."

With their flutes blasting and incessant drumming, the Joujouka tribe could really whip up a musical maelstrom, and Ahmed described the trancelike states their sound induced during the week long Feast of Boujeloud.

This village festival was dedicated to conjuring the spirit of Pan, who, so the story goes, originally bestowed the great gift of music on the village, in exchange for the love of their most beautiful woman. The villagers accepted, but traded the village idiot all dragged up instead. According to legend, a magnanimous Pan forgave their trickery, rid the idiot of his malady, and ever since the music has been regarded as a spiritual cure for mental illness. The festivities climaxed with the sacrificing of a goat. Once skinned, its hot, blood-soaked pelt was woven onto the shoulders of a village boy who, symbolising Pan, wore it as a cloak and danced like a dervish into the night. Ahmed added how this bloody climax apparently freaked Brian Jones out when he saw it, because he identified a little too closely with the slaughtered animal. For Kid, such talk was a feast for the imagination and he ate it up greedily.

Before he left Tangier, Ahmed gave Kid a rare photograph of himself as a handsome young man, dressed in a sharp, Italian suit, sitting at a restaurant table opposite Brian Jones, along with the London art dealer Robert Fraser, and their girlfriends. In the picture Fraser looks suitably cool, screwing the camera out from behind his dark shades, while Jones seems haunted, gazing out at the camera from beneath his sheep dog fringe. Studying Ahmed in the photo, Kid noted that, despite the passing years, you could see the courteous, shiny-eyed boy in the face of this now-distinguished gentleman.

The topic remained on music, as Ahmed spoke of his recent trip down the coast to Asilah with U2, where they filmed their video for *Mysterious Ways*. Kid, in turn, relayed an amazing tale about a musician friend of his who'd been part of the punk scene in London in the mid-70s. With his band, The Rejects, his mate had supported such second division punk acts as Chelsea, The Vibrators and Generation X. They'd also been booked to support The Sex Pistols and The Clash, but those gigs were cancelled when both bands got signed. His pal went on to play in countless new wave outfits, rubbing shoulders with Ian Dury and Chrissie Hynde. During that time, he lived with his girlfriend in a huge commune in Brixton, which had a thriving squat-scene.

They lived in Carlton Mansions on Coldharbour Lane, a gaunt, Victorian, clay coloured edifice, situated next to an overhead railway bridge. Over the years an unbelievable cast of characters passed through this residence, and a lot of bad, crazy shit went down. There were drug burns and OD's. A black, female singer friend of theirs threw herself off the roof, and when the Brixton riots broke out, right on their doorstep in the early eighties, rioters would often use the house as an escape route, jumping through the kitchen window to evade the police. Holes had been bored into the ceilings and floors so that each level could be accessed via ladders and everyone lived in each others' pockets.

It was against this backdrop that a female friend of his mate's dropped by one day and asked if he might tag along while she visited a medium at a Spiritualist church in Fulham. He accepted, but when they got there the medium immediately switched her attention away from the girl and honed in on him, with a warning that "black magick" was being practiced at his home. The woman then gave a full description of his Aussie biker landlord, describing the ever present Jackaroo hat he sported over his long, dark, Grebo hair, and his long, black straggly beard. She divined that the man was using dark forces to divide and conquer his tenants, and made reference to an "evil mural" that had been painted on the property, an explosive piece of information that completely blew his friend away. For it turned out the landlord had indeed recently contracted an artist to paint a mural of himself on the side of the building. He was depicted as a looming, satanic spectre, with spindly, stilt-like legs, bestriding a cityscape of London beneath him. As soon as his friend heard this bombshell it felt like a great weight had been lifted off his shoulders and, as if possessed, he rushed straight home and took a brush to the mural, and painted out his landlords feet, symbolically breaking the curse, although he didn't *consciously* realise this was what he was doing until later.

Soon after, the household broke up and they all went their separate ways. Interestingly, the mural is still there today, by stint of a preservation order, though it is now partly obscured by a towering plane tree. The landlords face has since been painted over and replaced by a death's head.

"Y'know, these communes never work out," Kid pithily concluded. "In the end people just get tired of clearing up other people's shit!"

Ahmed was engrossed in the story and got the significance of it instantly. All this talk of magick was getting to them, and as they sat there Ahmed began mimicking a patron who was sat smoking at the table in front of them, but had his back to them. As the man brought his kif pipe to his mouth and inhaled Ahmed aped him, drawing on his empty fingers and taking a deep lungful. Then, as the patron exhaled the hashish, a steady stream of smoke blew out of Ahmed's mouth at exactly the same time, and Kid gasped, "Wow," in amazement.

Night falls. A peacock strays off the manicured lawns in the grounds of the Forbes Mansion, and wanders into the sunken statue garden on the cliff top terrace. It hops onto a ledge, takes off and swoops down to the Cafe Hafa looking for scraps. Seen from behind it resembles a flying phantom, its magnificent, silken tail feathers ruffling like an exquisitely patterned Kabuki gown.

Showers of orange and white sparks pop and crackle, as a white wall on the outskirts of town crumbles into rubble. The hot coral sand on the beach illuminates itself against the star spangled sky. Kid stands on the bluff looking out at the warm, inviting sea, spread out like a shimmering, turquoise tapestry. The six-pointed star - the Seal of Solomon - from the Moroccan flag is superimposed on top of him.

Back in town the next day, Kid rounds a shadowy corner of the Kasbah and disappears. He re-emerges from a whitewashed bungalow at the end of a cul-de-sac, in the exclusive English suburb of Tangier. It's mid-morning and there's no one around. He starts jogging, in slow motion, along the middle of the street, passing the driveways of the bungalows on either side of him. As he jogs, the bright, clear sunshine casts his shadow on the smooth, freshly laid tarmac. Kid is intrigued to find that the sound around him has become muted for, as he listens down, he is unable to hear the pounding of his feet. All that can be heard is the faint sound of a cool breeze blowing gently through his hair.

As he turns a corner, Kid stumbles upon the bodies of his buddies, Bronx and Bomber, sprawled out on the sidewalk, both of them speared like lab mice, with huge dissecting pins the size of javelins. Their abdomens are sliced open, exposing their raw, splayed viscera. Electrodes are attached to their shorn heads, which have been shaved in such a slapdash, slipshod fashion, their scalps are splotched with clumps of hair and bald spots. The leads from the electrodes trail off and disappear through the slats of a louvered door that serves as a side entrance to a warehouse. Hidden behind the door is the nerve centre. A switch is flicked, and a bolt of electricity shoots through the electrodes. His pals writhe in agony, twitching and flinching spasmodically from the shock treatment, their faces twisted into tortured grimaces.

Kid opens the slatted door and enters, trying to find the power switch. The leads from the electrodes are bunched together with a cable tie, and he follows their trail until they disappear down a hole in the concrete floor to the basement.

He journeys through a walk-through alcove, and climbs some stone steps that lead up to the Tricorn Centre, a vast concrete monstrosity, annually voted the ugliest building in Britain. One of the worst examples of sixties brutalism, this notorious White City eyesore houses a shopping precinct, a nightclub and a multi-story car park. Kid ignores the lift and takes the staircase instead. He opens a door and finds himself in the empty nightclub. He walks across a deserted dance floor flashing with disco lights, leaves, and climbs a flight of subway steps. He emerges above ground and finds himself in the middle of Piccadilly Circus, standing under the statue of Eros – the beautiful patron saint of lust fulfilled, his arrow drawn and tipped with poison.

Seen from the rooftop of a terrace house, a row of backgardens taper off into the distance, framed under a lowering sky. The eerily still setting evokes and imparts a post-apocalyptic gloom. The leaves on the trees hang limp and damp from a recent downpour of toxic rain, the foliage the colour of deep bottle green, a *nuclear* green.

The dreams had obviously been inspired by his impending trip to London, but as Skyrise Kid woke it was those final, fading images that remained with him. They resonated with the dull, heavy lump of depression lying on his stomach, as immovable as a concrete paving slab. It was as if the depression had been nesting there, waiting for him to come to. He recollected his first curious encounter with this uniquely agonising state to which he now routinely succumbed.

It was the mid-seventies and he was six year old child living with his family in the top floor flat of Froxfield House in Landport, one of the roughest parts of White City, near the town centre. This was the Mort family home prior to moving to Somerstown. His mind travelled back to the stifling heat wave of 1976; Kid sits on the stoop of Froxfield House cheerfully murdering red ants. Crushing them beneath his fingertips, he scrapes them across the stone step leaving long, thin trails of red goo. A thick, pungent haze of mintweed hangs heavy on the air, and a tenant's radio plays a medley of hits: *Sing, Sing a Song, Y Viva Espana, Streets of London, Pearls a Singer,* the theme tune to *Black Beauty,* and Sailor's *Girls, Girls, Girls.*

Kid had awoken inexplicably early one morning in the poky bedroom he shared with Babs and Gemma. The room was still and unbearably quiet as the others slept, dead to the world. Daylight broke through a narrow crack in the curtains of the window, and as he looked out through the bedroom door to the hallway outside, the whole entire weight of the world came crashing down upon him. The deadening emptiness of that room, and his place in it, unleashed a tidal wave of depression that flooded his body, a monumental feeling of desolation and despair, so devastating in its force that it pinned him to the bed and actually began to feel euphoric. The whole bewildering experience wound up repeating itself many times over the years, albeit fleetingly, and with never the same impact or level of intensity as the original.

That was, until today.

As Skyrise Kid descended the well worn steps to the London underground station, he was struck by the thick, heavy miasma of fear that hung in the air. Anxiety gripped his already tense, nervous stomach. Black Astral dogs were patrolling. The dogs were a special breed of doberman pinschers that had attained a sixth sense ability to sniff out any guilty or incriminating behavior in humans. Today they were sweeping their canine radar across the subway system, trying to pick out suspects amongst the horde of travelling drones. Kid's nefarious visit to London had just gotten a whole lot worse.

Daunted by the beasts' presence, Kid shrunk away, trying to lose himself in the bustling crowd. He skulked behind one of the station's marble columns, surveying the dogs slyly, from a distance, careful not to make any eye contact with them. That was all it took, one sniff and they would detect he was up to no good.

A crowd of commuters was growing at the foot of the escalators, which had stalled temporarily due to some technical fault. Their ranks swollen by a steady stream of new arrivals, people jostled, unable to board the already packed steps, and he could feel the tension rising. Yet, despite the hustle and bustle, none of the passengers vent their grievances aloud. Indeed, those on the escalators remain perfectly calm, standing still as statues, two to a step, as they wait patiently for the escalators to start running again.

Nevertheless, Kid had a bad feeling about all this. An overwhelming sense of impending doom sat in his gut like sediment. Just then, out of the blue, came a blast from the past. A familiar face he hadn't seen in years cut through the swathe and made a beeline for him. Nick was a tall, reedy fellow with wispy hair and a high forehead. He was a real sweetheart kinda guy, and years ago they had been guitarists in the same rock band, but Kid was in no mood to reminisce and could barely muster a grimace.

Picking up on his old friend's distress, Nick asked why he was hiding out like this. "Because I'm shit scared of these dogs, man," Kid mumbled under his breath, trying not to look conspicuous. Before Nick could reassure him a commotion broke their conversation. Their attention was distracted to the prone, unconscious figure of a man, a derelict bum, sprawled flat out drunk on the floor, a puddle of vomit next to his head. The wino's inebriated body was blocking the entrance to a connecting tunnel, forcing travellers to step over him. Someone hadn't seen him in time and had tripped and fallen over the body, so hence all the noise.

Kid couldn't help but notice how much hair the drunk had, it was all straggly and matted and fell across his ruddy, weather beaten face. "It's funny innit," he mused to Nick, "how winos always have such thick heads of hair."

Everyone watched as an Astral dog approached the vagrant, its nose inspecting the full length of his body. From his booze-addled head to his filth-encrusted cagoule, along his urine-soaked tracksuit bottoms, down to his tattered sneakers where a sockless ankle flashed a manky leg, blue with dirt. The animal was midway through making the return journey when it stopped at a particular part of the man's leg. It gave a couple of tentative licks and Skyrise Kid cringed, he knew what was coming.

The dog set about the leg, tucking into the flesh. A sickening, squelchy sound filled the air as its salivating teeth gorged on subcutaneous tissue. Yellow liquid oozed out, and the fat fluid mixed with the blood seeping from the gaping wound. From the open gash you could see the severed tendons and arteries, and an ivory nub of marrow bone sticking out. Kid looked on in horror as the vile spectacle unfolded. Though the sight made him shudder, his morbid curiosity got the better of him and he was unable to tear his eyes away. He couldn't *not* look.

Zoning

Muffled screams swept through the nauseous onlookers, trying desperately to stifle their noise so as not to draw attention to themselves. It seemed the deeper the dog's jaws sunk into the wino's flesh, the more ravenous its appetite became, and soon it was stripping chunks of gristle from both legs. It was only then that the tramp began to stir from his drunken stupor. Lifting his groggy head from the floor, he lurched forward, his blurry eyes straining to focus on his surroundings. There was a slight delay in his reaction, followed by a chilling, high-pitched shriek as he looked down to find himself being eaten alive. His horror-stricken face, twisted into a hideous mask conveying all the excruciating agony. His wide, crazed eyes bore the unforgettable look of somebody who knows they are about to die horribly. As he screamed, silver trails of spit dribbled out of the corners of his mouth. Panicking, he jerked his upper body back and forth, trying in vain to wrestle his lower half away, but it was all too late. Other Astral dogs were already converging on him to feast.

The tramp's face turned purple, straining from the slaughter being wreaked upon him. He convulsed, apoplectic, and after a series of involuntary, spasmodic jolts, his heart gave out. Looking up and out into the middle distance, as if staring beyond it all, his eyes glazed over and death closed in. You could physically see the life force go out in his face, as if some inner light had been switched off. His head hit the floor with a bone-jarring crack, and a clotted glob of blood flobbed out of his mouth, followed by the wheezing of a long drawn out death rattle.

The dogs buried their heads in the fresh corpse's stomach, lunching on the intestines, spleen, purple organs and viscera. Gnawing upwards, they eviscerated the torso, crunching up the bones of the rib cage, the rind of the skin serrated by their teeth marks all the way from the sternum to the abdomen. While they lapped up all the remnants of the foul spillage,

104

the malodorous stench of human drek putrefied the air.

For a moment a disquieting hush settled over the station, punctuated by the sound of sobbing from shaken passengers, unable to contain their composure any longer. Some squeamish commuters had already thrown up, while others huddled together, comforting one another. Then scuffles began breaking out over by the escalators. What started as grumblings soon swelled to a clamour as the crowd began to perceive the very real threat of a crush occurring. A mounting sense of desperation began to take hold. The place felt like a pressure cooker ready to blow.

Skyrise Kid remained rooted to the spot, paralysed with fear, his outline buzzing with horror. For the first time in his life he experienced that special kind of fear you only ever see in cartoons, the kind that wobbles your belly from the inside. As he turned away from the grisly melee, he was cut dead in his tracks. Casting his eyes downwards, everything seemed to grind down to a terrifying slow motion. There before him, he met the waiting glare of an Astral dog, it's hackles raised, it's red, glowering eyes boring into his, brimming with unremitting hate.

CHAPTER 7
SNUFF TV

Astral Boy wanders across the stone shingle rooftop of a warehouse building in the meat packing district near Greenwich Village. Across the Hudson River, he can make out the New Jersey docks and waterfront through the hazy afternoon distance. On the rooftop, half buried in the shingle, are what looks like a collection of large, ornately decorated, Faberge eggs. Each egg has a fuse sticking out of it. They are actually elaborate firecrackers, ready to be lit by the residents of Chinatown to ward off evil spirits and keep trespassers away.

In the fast, fading light of dusk, shadows fall across a row of bombed-out brownstones in Alphabet City. Inside one of the derelict premises, amid all the filth and squalor, a Native American Chief, resplendent in his feather headdress, lounges chest deep in a sunken bath filled with murky brown water. There is a horrible stench of damp in the air, like coffee gone bad. Paint flakes off the walls, the floorboards littered with garbage and drug paraphernalia: yellowing newspapers, syringes, blackened spoons and the ceramic shards of a broken toilet bowl amongst the detritus. The Chief reclines, stony faced, blank eyes fixed to the TV set in front of him. He is watching *SNUFF TV*, a twenty-four hour "anything goes" cable channel, broadcast out of New Jersey.

The first clip is footage of a horrific torching taken from a CCTV camera overlooking the busy concourse of New York's Penn Station. Four black youths target a random female commuter. Zeroing in on the victim, they each douse her with lighter fluid, set her alight, and then scatter like rats in all directions. Fellow commuters back away from the burning woman who flails around frantically, before some brave man approaches and tamps out the flames with his jacket.

The next segment opens with an aerial view of the glossy beachfronts of Miami. The camera zeroes in on a confection of pastel coloured condos in the Little Havana district. Inside the kitchens of one of the apartments, rays of sunlight stream across a shiny linoleum floor. A kooky, gaunt-faced, hippy chick with long, black hair parted down the middle, turns to a little boy stripped to the waist. She looms over him, clearly insane, spitting curses in hysterical, scattergun Spanish. As she shrieks, she scribbles the incantations down onto a note pad in front of her. Once a page is completed, she rips the sheet off its spine and hurls the hex at the terrified child, symbolically defiling him with its contents. The poor, little mite flinches as she does this, bewildered by his mother's aberrant behavior. His bottom lip curled, his teary eyes search her face, imploring her to stop.

A delicate, snow white baby goat is pushed into the kitchen by unseen hands, its spindly legs skittering across the slippery floor. Tottering on all fours, the creature looks unsure of its new surroundings. The whacked-out witch sweeps the startled animal off it's feet and cradles it in her arms, rocking it back and forth in a warped display of mock, maternal affection. She stares maniacally with a deranged, shit-eating grin on her face. When the goat fidgets and scrambles to get loose, she tightens her grip and lifts its chin with her left hand. Surreptitiously, she draws a carving knife from behind her back with her other hand and slashes the animal's throat, splattering her son with the sacrificial blood. The terrorised boy cowers on his knees, his hands over his head, screeching as his unhinged mother delights in anointing him with the mucky ooze.

This is followed by a scene from a European porno starring Skyrise Kid. It opens with the cobbled streets of Prague, viewed by Kid from his coach window as he and his fellow passengers travel through the city, en route to their hotel. The tour guide points out the plaque marking the building where Franz Kafka was born, as well as the grim looking offices where he worked as an insurance clerk.

A slim chambermaid shows Kid to his hotel room. She is in her mid-twenties with dark, gypsy features. The room is sparsely furnished, just a single bed, wardrobe and a chest of drawers. The maid hangs Kid's coat in the closet, and then bends over the bed to fix the sheets. Kid quietly moves in on her while she has her back to him. Threading his arms under her oxters he clasps her tightly to his chest. She gasps as she is taken unawares, but after the initial shock, the girl melts and relaxes into his arms. From behind, Kid kneads her teeny tits through the rough material of her unflattering uniform. His right hand drops down and burrows between her legs, rubbing her cunt. The maid's head falls back on his shoulder and she moans with pleasure, her groans growing louder and more heated as he works her pussy with his right hand and squeezes her tits with the other.

Dirty Sue materialises on the bed like a pulchritudinous vision, that sumptuous body squeezed into a black, whale-boned corset, her legs in fishnets and thigh-high boots. Lying seductively on her side, she runs her hands seductively over her body, watching the sex play in progress. Kid's eyes lock onto hers. Her gaze lingers then switches to study the facial expressions breaking across the maid's face, who is still unaware of her presence. She just continues to writhe at Kid's fingertips, murmuring to his touch. Sue raises herself from the bed, jiggling in all the right places. She scoops out her stupendous tits and lets them hang over the top of her basque. Kid leers at her with a dirty grin. Sue smiles and closes in on the maid who becomes stuck in the middle of a sex sandwich. Startled at first, she soon picks up the action, and starts undulating between them. Kid reaches out and grabs a handful of Sue's tit, squashing the maid as he suckles hard on her nipple. Sue then takes the lead. Lowering herself, she rubs her incredible rack up and down the maid's body, overwhelming the slender, young thing with her behemoth bust. There is a jump cut, and the footage comes to an abrupt end with Sue pointing at the bed. The camera follows the direction of her finger and ends with a close up of the bed sheets, splattered with long, silvery threads of spunk.

The raunch is replaced by a clip from a BBC documentary about drug psychosis in teenagers. It shows real life footage of a suicidal girl taken during her therapy session, her head bowed, her long, lank, greasy hair obscuring a face wet with tears. Sobbing, she can only speak in fragments. "My flesh… has this stench… it smells like dog flesh."

Another clip, plucked out of the BBC archives, plays. It's an old public information film from the seventies about rail safety, warning kids of the dangers of playing near a railway track. Filmed on a railway line in the depths of the English countryside, a group of school children, dressed in white tee shirts and shorts, march straight into a railway tunnel and disappear inside. Moments later, there is an awful screeching sound as a train roars through the tunnel, but is unable to brake in time. The intimation is that most of the unseen kids have been killed instantly on impact, but gradually some blood stained survivors file out of the tunnel, hobbling and traumatised. This footage of them dissolves, replaced by images showing dead bodies being stretchered out by ambulance men.

Next up, is a teaser from an arty, French porn movie. A starlet made up to look like Madonna is spotlit in a darkened room. Naked and spread-eagled on her back, she is strapped into some kind of mechanical fuck machine, a red ball-gag stuffed in her mouth. This Meccano looking contraption is equipped with soft metal levers that have "pleasure balls" attached to the end of them. The cooze demonstrates how, by gyrating her body, she can control these levers and manipulate the pleasure balls into her orifices. Gradually she works up a steam and gets the rickety rig going, and with the aid of a close up, you can see one of the balls working its way into her pussy. She writhes, licking her lips, her flesh rippling as though being fucked by a real man. As she huffs and puffs and fucks herself stupid, sexually suggestive dialogue spoken by Madonna in the movie *Body of Evidence* plays over and over on a tape loop.

This is followed by some undercover police footage following two suspects believed to be part of an animal torture ring run out of Saint Paul, Minnesota. Shot from inside a surveillance van, two white males with ponytails walk down the stoop of their apartment building and get into a car. The undercover cops tail them to a lock up. Inside, they are filmed covertly by hidden cameras as they release two german shepherds from a metal cage. The dogs are lifted and strung up by their collars on meat hooks in the ceiling. They wriggle and kick out, howling and whimpering, and as they hang there, choking, the men use them as punch bags, pummeling them with their fists. They then pull out knives and begin stabbing the dogs repeatedly. They slit their throats, severing the jugular, sawing through the tendons until the heads come off, and the decapitated dogs drop like sacks of potatoes to the floor.

This all too real reality gives way to a grotesque tableau, set on the side of a desert road. Looking like pilgrims who just stepped off the *Mayflower*, a maniacal preacher man and his wife grease the appallingly blistered skin of their naked amputee daughter. The young woman has only stumps for arms and legs, and as her parents cradle her in their arms, they cry out blessings to Jehovah.

"Oh Lord, in all Your infinite wisdom and glory, You have seen fit to strike down this accursed creature, this vile abomination," the fanatical father says.

"Amen," chimes his dour, bonnet-headed bint. The poor girl looks close to death, but as the bible-thumpers work themselves up into a religious fervour they accelerate the roughness of their rub down, oblivious to her torment.

Pictures coming through static interference ..... The television snow clears and opens on the interior of the launderette across the road from the Kings Theatre in White City. The premises are being used after hours as the set for a porno shoot, shot guerrilla-style by Geoff and Dirty Sue. Masturbating furiously, Skyrise Kid shoots his wad across the glass of a KISS pinball machine. A topless glamour girl enters the frame wearing a pleated, Burberry cheerleader skirt, white bobbysox and red 'fuck me' pumps, her mousy hair in pigtails. The saucy minx drapes her lithe, sapling body on the glass and laps the cum up from it. As she does, her knickerless keister moons the camera, the pink slit peeking out beneath her crack. She smears her peachy tits on the glass, wiping the sperm around as she slides across the slippery surface. Using a clever camera trick, the nymphet is shot from beneath a separate pane of glass, creating the illusion that it is the glass covering the pinball machine. She smiles coquettishly as she squashes her spunk-smeared tits up against it.

Finally, there's some more undercover police footage, this time taken by the New York City Vice Squad. Shot from the rear seat of a surveillance car, the clip centres on skid row where three Bowery bums sit on a sidewalk curb with their feet in the gutter. Two oldtime winos flank their bag-lady chum. A bald, middle-aged businessman approaches a black pimp slouched outside a liquor store just behind them. The pimp is dressed in a long, black, leather trench coat and rocks a matching black *Down with OPP* ski hat. The businessman has a word in the pimp's ear and, after a couple of conciliatory nods, the pimp wanders over to the sozzled trio and passes some instructions on to them, out of earshot. The pimp returns and nods to the bald man who shoots him a $50 bill. The hoary, old bag lady pulls herself up from the curb, turns around, and greets the bald trick as he approaches her. Falling to her knees, she unzips the man's pinstripe pants, takes out his weighty, flaccid cock, and in broad daylight, starts administering a messy, slobbering blow job. Stirred by her activity, the rummies turn around and begin to hitch up the many layers of her raggedy clothing. Lifting through the rolls of cardigans and shawls wrapped around her waist, they peel down her vile vestments and spank her wrinkly ass, snuffling their drunken snouts in her manky drawers.

A taxi cab makes its way through the deserted, morning streets of dull, grey London. It cruises down a uniform row of wartime terrace houses, the kind still found in the backwaters around Waterloo train station. The cab crawls up to the curb and drops Skyrise Kid off outside the address where the connection lives. He rings the doorbell and waits and a few moments later the neo-nazi answers and lets him in. They shake hands cordially, and Kid sizes him up. He is a rangy, hollow-cheeked young man, with slate grey eyes and short, sandy hair, parted at the side. He could be a public-school boy. As they talk in the hall, he comes across as polite and shy and gives off an archetypal loner vibe. Kid can sense the guy is relieved to have finally found someone whom he believes shares his secret passion.

A grim, sepulchral atmosphere entombs the residence. It is like going from day to night, as the guy leads Kid through a darkened passage into a dismally lit living room where the curtains are drawn and the only light comes from the blue glare of the television set.

The young man offers Kid his armchair seat, then kneels on the floor in front of the VCR to rewind the videotape Kid has come all this way to see. It is only then that Kid notices the guy's fat, hard-faced mother, whom he only sensed as a vague ambiguous presence, but hadn't seen properly until now. He can just make her out through the flickering light of the television set. Sat in stony silence on the settee over in the shadows to his left, she's a fearsome looking harridan. She eyes him suspiciously, emitting cold, matriarchal indignation. The matronly hausfrau is dressed in a sleeveless pinafore that exposes her burly arms. Her yellow hair done up in French braid, her stern, beetred face suggests she suffers from high blood pressure; in fact she looks plain fit to burst. Kid wasn't expecting an audience and figures she indulges her son, but doesn't necessarily approve of all this.

As if the horror at the subway yesterday hadn't been bad enough, Kid now has to contend with the family dog, a german shepherd - typical - which wanders in and sniffs him over. Kid views the beast with sneering contempt and shoots it a baleful look. He was especially leery of alsatians, having been mauled by one as a kid, but as a guest in a stranger's house he was in an awkward position. Feeling all eyes were on him, Kid forced himself to endure it's attentions, for a while at least. The animal is playful, at first, and tries to ingratiate itself in the slimy way dogs do, simpering and wagging its tail, baring it's teeth, and nudging it's cold, damp nose into the palm of his hand. Kid's gut curdles at that, and using that same hand he gives the dog a half-hearted rub on the head, wiping the moisture off on it's coat. Regrettably, this only encourages the fucker to bury it's head in his lap. This gets Kid all agitated, but he's reluctant to say anything at first, and instead he fires his host a withering look, hoping he'll call the animal off...he doesn't and the dog gets even friskier, until Kid's hand recoils with a wince when a lick turns into a nip.

Incensed, he flips out and rounds on the guy, "Hey, man, d'ya think you could get your dog off me?" The dude apologises and drags the animal away by the collar, kicking it out the room. Finally, they settle down to watch the video. To the sound of a film projector whirring, titles appear on a black screen: *DEATH CAMP TAPES.*

A class of around forty prepubescent school children file into a communal shower room that has toilet stalls running down the side of the far wall. The chambers are sterile and bare, and there's a lingering smell of gas coming from the vents in the ceiling. A cadaverous looking SS officer with horn-rimmed glasses enters the room. He walks down the row of toilet cubicles. With slow deliberation he swings open each door, the creek of its hinges heightening the suspense that he may find the shivering presence of some terrified child cowering inside. With his severe, saturnine manner, he cuts a menacing figure. His imposing, black uniform, so calculatingly sinister in its conception, made all the more striking in these stark, white surroundings. The children collect glockenspiels from a wicker trunk and line up like a choir in four rows, rubbertipped mallets in hands.

The makeshift orchestra launches into the haunting chimes of *September Song*: "Oh, it's a long, long while from May to December, but the days grow short when you reach September..."

The scene shifts to the muddy prison yard outside. Judging from the breath billowing from the soldiers' mouths, it is a bitterly cold winter's morning. Filmed from a gun tower, we look down on two parallel lines of prisoners, a dozen on either side, buried up to their necks in mud so that only their heads are visible, resting like footballs on the surface. It soon becomes apparent that the barbaric purpose behind them facing each other is so one line of pitiful prisoners is forced to watch the gruesome execution of the others, knowing full well the same thing will shortly be happening to them. The prisoners are manacled at the neck by an iron collar, and are shackled to one another by a length of chain that lays slackened in the mud. A guard gives the order and the chains are whipped up off the ground, sprung taut by an overhead pulley. The propulsion wrenches off the prisoners heads, popping them like champagne corks. Headless torsos are dredged up through the slurry by the sheer force, and in slow motion, a decapitated body is shown bobbing around in the mire.

More sordid atrocities follow. This time the chains are tied under the oxters of a naked prisoner who is only half buried in the mud. When the chains are sprung, they rip the arms out of their sockets, spraying blood everywhere, the poor man's trunk is left rocking back and forth from the tremendous exertion.

In the next clip, a naked woman is marched down a line of fellow female prisoners who kneel in the mud, their hands behind their heads. In what appears to be a sick game for her life, she is forced to stab each one of her fellow inmates in the face with a butcher knife.

The final ghastly segment is a grainy black and white

clip, shot inside an austere prison barracks. Although the film is silent, the constant whirring sound of the camera is audible throughout. The footage has obviously been shot at night, as the dormitory is cast in half-light. As the camera backpedals down a row of shelf-like bunks, it shines it's lens on the skeletal prisoners sleeping five to a tier. Unaware they are being filmed, they lay on top of each other, their bodies tangled up in uncomfortable heaps.

The camera moves away from these cramped quarters, and halts as it arrives at a single cot at the viewer's end of the dorm. From the foot of the bed it concentrates on a quivering, shaven-headed prisoner wearing obligatory stripped holocaust pajamas.

A venal looking SS officer stands over him, berating the man, for the cruel and heartless amusement of his fellow officers watching from the sidelines. An unseen, solitary lamp illuminates the bed in a sinister, oval glow. The SS brute strongarms the poor wretch, squeezing him tightly by the nape of the neck, forcing his face into the putrid smelling bed sheets, soiled with the body odours left behind by a multitude of previous occupants. The officer pulls the sheet out from under him, and proceeds to wipe it roughly on the arse of a fellow prisoner who has been turfed out of his bunk. Petrified and humiliated, this second prisoner grovels, wilting in the wings to the right of shot. The officer returns to the single cot and thrusts the feces-stained bedding back into the abused prisoner's face. The helpless man thrashes his head from side to side, trying frantically to pull back away from the sheet, but there is just no strength in his feeble, emaciated body and his struggle proves fruitless. In the end, he is shown retching in disgust and curled up in a fetal position, his abhorrence so alarmingly clear that it manages to convey itself, even though the film is silent.

A paralytic prisoner is carried down the aisle of the barracks in the arms of a butch German guard. His withered body is all crooked and bent out of shape, due to the prolonged lack of sleeping space. He is taken down to the single cot where he is brutally dumped. You can make out the man's agonising screams as his crippled frame bounces painfully on the hard mattress. The SS officer is shown in close-up for once, spitting some kind of orders at the first prisoner on the floor, and in an excessively threatening manner, he extends his forearm, pointing to his new, decrepit bedfellow.

It soon becomes clear what his final debasement will be, as the man begins to crawl uneasily upon his fellow prisoner's twisted, defenseless body. Fumbling in his pants, he reaches for his limp cock, and attempts to straddle him. He stops, unable to bring himself to carry out the rape, and beseeches his cold-hearted captors, pleading for the crude barbarity to end. Scornful of such snivelling eyewash, the officer responds by drawing his lugar from his belt, and placing it to the prisoner's temple. The closing shot shows the broken man capitulating, spasmodically humping the old frail, while his sadistic persecutors jeer, goading him on.

CHAPTER 8
LSD JACKET

In a blacked out, strobe lit room, Astral Boy sits in the centre of a magick circle, the sacred names of Lucifer, Nuit, Hadit, Ra Hoor Kuit, Chaos, Babalon and Lilith inscribed around the rim. Holding a blue disk bearing Aleister Crowley's *Mark of the Beast* symbol in one hand, Astral Boy jacks off with the other, firing up the Kundalini energy at the base of his spine. Dressed in a dark jumpsuit, he lays face down, his head, hands and feet aligned to the five points of the pentagram. Suddenly he levitates and hovers in the air, his knees bent, his hands gripping his ankles as he strikes a skydiver's pose. He floats back down gracefully to the floor and switches position, from starshape to crabshape, and starts scuttling round the circle like a crustacean. He ends the ritual sitting shirtless in lotus position, wearing a black Ku Klux Klan type hood and making the Baphomet "as above so below" hand signal. A large, blue flame flickers above his head. All of a sudden it ignites, and with a flash Astral Boy explodes into sparks like a Roman candle.

Séance pranks break out. Crystal balls fog up and shatter, showering fragments of space and time. Runes are cast then cast aside. Voodoo dolls come apart at the seams and holy books turn to dust at the touch of his hands. Catholic saints fall on their swords, hoisted by their own petard, and the house of tarot cards slides off its foundations. Ouija boards spell out ... THE END.

Spellbound, Astral Boy comes to with the symbol of the swastika spinning inside his head. He is surprised to find he has been taken back to the Spiritualist temple in Southsea. The hall is in total disarray, like some kind of maelstrom has hit it. Chairs are upended, his clothes are in tatters, and there's an overwhelming scent of burnt candle wax in the air. The magickal working had lit a fuse at the core of his being. His whole body was charged up. Bull-necked, his arms flexed rigid in a bodybuilders "pincer" pose. Muscles he never knew he had ripped and bulged across his back, torso and biceps. He was in possession of a bestial strength. He felt like he could shit steel.

Suddenly, two beams of white light shoot out from his eye sockets and orange sparks fire out his mouth. Astral Boy levitates six feet off the ground as strobe lights flicker in the third eye, embedded in the dead centre of his forehead. He boasts a raging hard-on and showers of white sparks spontaneously ejaculate from his cock.

He is filmed against a blue screen upon which a series of images and backdrops are projected: the arresting skyline of Manhattan... the blasted heath of a desertscape... a back alley in Tangier... photographs fluttering across a rubble strewn wasteland... a rain slicked street in Alphabet City... an exquisite sunken statue garden... the concrete jungles of Somerstown... a black office building with tinted blue windows, so ominous it hums... a huge close-up of a petrified dragonfly suspended in amber...

Beautiful, white gossamer wings sprout between Astral Boy's shoulder blades, puncturing the skin. His wings open wide as an electronic advertisement hoarding in Times Square flashes up on the screen behind him, displaying the words. in dazzling neon lights:

RESURRECTION ON 84th STREET OF ANGEL HGA .

By the time he was twenty, Skyrise Kid had already left home and moved into his own place down by the seafront. He still kept in touch with his family regularly, and dropped by one evening, unannounced, to collect the flight jacket he left behind on his last visit.

Letting himself in through the backdoor, he went upstairs to where he knew everyone would be. It was as he reached the top of the stairs that he was struck by a tangible presence of evil pervading the upper landing, a seedy, musty, earthiness that tainted the atmosphere.

At the top of the stairs, directly in front of him, the door to his uncle's bedroom was wide open. Kid looked in on Ryland, who, as ever, was lying on his side on his bed, reclining like an old opium smoker *on the hip*, smoking a fag and watching TV. His resigned features lit by the electric blue glare of the television set. Initially unaware of his nephew hovering at his door, Ryland sat up with a start, "Hello son, alright?" As always he was wearing his striped, cotton pajama bottoms and a food stained shirt.

Kid explained that he had come to pick up his jacket, and after planting a tender kiss on his nephew's cheek, Ryland hurriedly shuttled downstairs to fetch it from the cubby-hole, leaving Kid with the impression that he wanted to bundle him out of the house as quickly as possible.

Roused by their voices, Babs emerged from her bedroom and met him in the middle of the landing, greeting him in a hushed whisper. Because of her ordinarily amiable disposition, Kid was surprised to find how anxious and on edge she was. She seemed on tenterhooks, wound up with worry, yet desperately trying to put on a brave front... at this she failed miserably. Babs' face was an open book, and the tense, vexed look in her eyes betrayed her. She motioned her nephew towards her, as if she had some secret news to impart. As Kid stepped forward, the door to Nan's old bedroom opened suddenly and the malevolent force responsible for his relative's odd, skittish behaviour, made himself known. Babs blanched and froze stock still, the colour visibly draining in her face.

Kid assumed the swarthy stranger to be a new lodger, but as this belligerent bull of a man barged between them, he exuded a diabolical menace. He possessed the brooding aura of an old style gangster, complete with jet black, slicked-back hair, and requisite five o'clock shadow. His hard, glowering eyes scowled daggers at Kid, who could feel the spiky hate prickling off him. The man made his was way to the bathroom at the end of the landing.

Just as the guy closed the door behind himself, Ryland rushed up the stairs and handed Kid his jacket, almost tripping over the laundry basket in the corner. It was then, as they were all gathered together under the dim landing light, that Kid noticed how spaced-out his aunt and uncle were. Though they were striving to maintain a grip on things, their pupils were pinned, and Kid realised they'd both unwittingly been drugged by the stranger and kept in this doped state over a prolonged period of time. Still suffering from hallucinations, they were seeing the devil incarnate as he really was, and not in the gangster guise that Kid had witnessed.

Before any questions could be asked or any answers sought, Kid eased himself into his jacket and - WHOOSH - he was hit by an electric shock as LSD blasted his spirit out of his body-shell, and the mind screen behind his eyes exploded with a blinding series of camera flashes that filled the room in silver-white brilliance.

The LSD blew open a Pandora's box, unleashing a barrage of deep-seated images and multi-sensory experiences that blitzkrieged his senses. Time travelling along memory lines, he was transported by an intense nostalgia for people, places and times revisited. As though thrown into a future/past life, he recognised familiar faces he had never seen before. A large family gathered in front of a barrel shaped Gypsy caravan and waved at him as if posed for a family photograph; ancestors so familiar and yet never met, reunited in an all too brief moment.

He began testing different strengths of thoughts and trying them out. Thoughts were water pouring into a bucket until it overflows and tips, spilling its contents into another empty pail below, like a schematic flow diagram brought to life. This trickle-down effect was shown in action and Kid watched, entranced, as the last bucket of thought is thrown away at the moment of death.

There was a complete synaesthesia of the senses - hearing colours, tasting sounds. Grey sinus taste of breathing tubes and incubators… sweet coconut smell of Spanish beaches… bright, crisp sunlight cast across a deserted school playground on a cold winters morning… the summer scent of freshly cut grass on an aerodrome. In the back of his mouth: the taste of liquorice, cherry popsicles, vegetable soup and sweet *Jack Daniels*.

For a moment Kid was on Trebovir Road in Earls Court, London. A tree lined street cast in shadowy light that possesses a dream-like quality. He sees a sepia tinted vision of Victorian London: drunkards spilling out of spit and sawdust pubs, tramps laying in the gutter, smashed and washed up against the terminus of Victoria Station. The scene shifts to some faraway beach where, above muddy sea waters, birds take flight, soaring into a red sky: "To think we are their masters beggars belief."

The blue sparks from a cooker's ignition fire off behind his eyes. Kid gets turned on by a sexy mirage of a slutty, punk rock chick dressed all trashy, in a black leather skirt and torn fishnet stockings. A walking phallus in the mind's eye. Being and nothingness.....

It was like testing out reality by dipping your toe in the bath water to check the temperature. Kid mentally jumped into a weird jungle. A monstrous blown-up image of a hideous insect - himself - as a praying mantis seen magnified through the lens of a camera, that is what he felt like. Red devils skulking in the branches of trees, grinning like Cheshire cats. Riding the U-Bahn through Berlin, gazing at statues of mummified corpses half-buried in the subway tunnel walls. Visions of sun kissed angels lit up inside. Golden faced geriatrics with glorioles around their heads, all radiant and serene with beatific beams, brilliantine hair and Florida tans. Kid remembers the wise words of Ahmed his guide in Tangier, "Evil swirls and rushes around your feet, as angels fly up and down taking messages."

Crashing and falling inside... "God is ineffable, beyond our ken. Our minds are not able to grasp or fully comprehend the enormity of what he is."

Hanging onto words for an indeterminate period of time, dwelling on long sounds. Lost in folds of LSD time. The fingers inside his head just...miles away. Talking to himself, watching himself doing the actions. Thoughts and images coming in from this other place, as though dictated straight into his mind. Leaving messages on a special highway: "We are only an outward show, a shell. What's wrapped inside is far more important. You're the writer, the actor, the cameraman, the director, the star in the film of you're life. *Zoning* is the name of the film of your life."

Kid clasped his tremulous hands to his humming head, and ran his fingers through his long hair, soft as silk to the touch. His hands slipped through his scalp and sunk into the mash of his brain, like mushy peas and gravy. There is a terrible moment of realisation as Kid finds he has no control over his mind, in fact his all-powerful mind is overriding him. He was no longer able to control the overwhelming flow of thoughts. His mind was tormenting him, scaring him to death. You could disappear into the mind and never come back again. His wound nerves really wringing it out now. Hell in your veins, *helling* your veins. He had to get out.

Panicked, Kid clambered back down the stairs, licked by flames from the burning banisters, but as he reached to bottom he was assailed by another series of blinding white camera flashes... CAMERAS CAN'T COME OFF NOW... CAMERA'S CAN'T COME OFF... LOSING IT... SHAKING BADLY... NOW IN DISTORTION NO EXIST... NO EXITS... HEAD BURNING ME... ME... ME...TAKE THE CAMERAS AWAY... TAKE THE CAMERAS AWAY.

Kid wakes and finds himself on the beach at the seafront, the sound of waves lapping against the shore. As he staggers along the coastline, bombed-out, he spies an attractive, young couple up ahead. Kid sidles up to them, but they remain unaware of his presence. They're completely enraptured in each other, caught up in a world of their own, far away. The goth girl is a pretty, willowy thing. Her crimped, orange hair tumbling around her porcelain pale face, decorated in Egyptian eye makeup. She wears a long, flowing, velveteen dress that falls all the way to her feet. Her boyfriend is older and possessed of moody rockstar looks. He has black, shoulder length, corkscrew hair and is squeezed into a tight pair of black jeans, ripped at the knees. A beat-up, leather jacket completes his look. As the delicate girl nestles her head in her boyfriend's lap, he leans back on the stones, resting on his elbows, gazing out to sea. The grey waters reflect the overcast sky, and South Parade Pier looms in the background behind them. Under the pier, a yellow, foam sludge floats on the surface of the water, the spume congealed from cooking fats that have been flushed down the drains from the kitchen in the restaurant above. The greasy spew stinks to high heaven and leaves a ring of scum around the legs of the wooden stanchions.

The fur trimmed hood of Kid's jacket has a zipper running down the middle, which when undone, splits the hood in two so that each part hangs off his shoulders like fuzzy epaulets. Burning up, Kid slips out of the jacket and instantly it is as if the backdrop of a stage production descends from the rafters to slot in place, right in front of him. The extravagantly-lavish set is straight out of *The Arabian Nights*, and Kid is now privy to what the young lovers have been seeing all along. Reclining on a bed of sumptuous cushions, the lovers luxuriate in a Bedouin tent, preening like silent matinee idols; the man now coolly attired in a white, cotton robe and matching headscarf, his glammed up girlfriend wearing a see-through slip and a golden headdress. A harem of sultry, scantily clad handmaidens cater to their every whim, feeding the couple honey-dipped dates, and fanning them with giant palm leaves. The lush, exotic scene sizzles with an erotic sensuality.

In the diary he began writing after he left the drug rehab, Skyrise Kid recorded what happened next: "I woke up to a hyperventilating hell. Shocking jolts of pain zinging down the tracks of my inner arms. Nerves ringing from the intensity, jarring me back into consciousness. I was suffocating in the throes of a panic attack. My mind speeding out of control, as though some higher power had pressed its foot down hard on an accelerator pedal inside my head. Scrambling, unable to catch a breath, the panic escalates, feeding on itself. My hands shaking, my arms aching from the unremitting pressure and excruciating pain. My nerves tightening with the tension, like over-tuned guitar strings ready to snap. All my senses racing, panic screaming like a siren in my stomach. I had lost all the apparatus of self control, as though the safety bars of my central nervous system had been lifted up and off me, turning my viscera to jelly, and leaving a tangle of broken body strings. My head was being squeezed in an ever-tightening vice, and dreadful, nasty, burning sensations flared up inside it. A searing heat, like sunburn under the skull, scorching my brainpan, inflaming my ear and right side of my face. The temples pulsing relentlessly on either side of my whirring head. I flinched and winced as I endured the repeated twinges along my hairline. It was as if that steel hook implement, used by hairdressers to draw strands of hair through a perforated rubber skullcap to highlight them, was pulling out the hairs along my hairline, except the hairs were being pulled down through the follicles on my scalp, leaving only a cold, steel air of baldness in their place. Each successive, irrevocable twinge of hair loss inducing an instantaneous welling of hopelessness and despair in my stomach.

"I get another dose of the horrors that shivers across the back of my shoulders, bristling the hairs on the nape of my neck and the back of my head. Wet, schizophrenic droplets of LSD - a toxic fallout of *real* acid rain - falling *onto* then *into* my smarting head, trickling down my face, as my mind melts in rivulets. A mind tormenting me, ravaging me, scaring me to death.

"Sensitivities so acute, I became schizophrenically aware of my body. I could feel it so intensely, *living* on me. Trapped inside this thin prison, my skeleton an inner spiking stand with sharp points piercing my insides, hitting all the pressure points, the nubs of the glands in my throat swelling up, blocking my airway. My windpipe seemed to have disappeared, so that every time I swallowed it felt like the saliva in my mouth was squeezed down painfully over my adams apple before emptying onto my rib cage.

"Air squeezed out of the side of my neck like a balloon deflating, and it felt as though I had wooden blocks lodged under my oxters, so that my arms were unable to hang down comfortably by my sides. There was an awful sensation that felt like I had pencils inserted into my ears, that threatened to puncture the drum, and stigmata pains throbbed in the palms of my hands, as if burning nails had been hammered into them. God, I felt exactly like the guy on the cover of the book, *Scanners*.

"Sucking for air, I was seized by the dreadful fear of imminent death. That devastating realisation that it's all boiled down to this, these final moments. Living from second to second. You always wonder how, where and when your death will come and this was it. This is what death feels like. Death had jumped on my rails, and come upon me. My death was happening now."

CHAPTER 9
FLY UP AND GO BALD

Frantic images from inside a deserted, ramshackle mansion, seen through the eyes of an unseen entity hurtling at full speed down a long, dim lit corridor. It's like a ghost train ride, as the entity veers right sharply when it reaches the end of the corridor. Blasting through double doors, it careens up two flights of stairs and along a creepily-tilted upper landing, stopping with a jolt outside the door of the attic room.

Skyrise Kid cranks a hypodermic needle into his vein with a slow burning sting. The silent soar of heroin sates his stomach and curls his toes back, surrounding his body in a warm, orange *Ready Brek*glow. Wrapped in it's cozy cocoon, all cares and concerns melt away, his spirit lifting off him like cigarette smoke swirling up to the ceiling. Glinting silver flashes flicker like silent lightening, shattering Kid's mind's eye. He is sucked up into a twisting black vortex, riding a high-speed subway in the sky, hurtling through deserted stations that flash by like flicker frames of memories.....

The action moves to the strobe-lit interior of the middle garage in the Oldbury House car park. With each strobe flicker the hooded cultists of Tabeth Ali are illuminated by a flash of light. They are conducting a baptism of hellfire on a semiconscious Skyrise Kid who is laid out on a makeshift altar. Kid can feel a demonic presence vibrating his being, strumming across the jangled body strings of his nervous system. An overhead shot shows Kid's somnambulant body, his eyes flickering beneath their lids in the REM stage of sleep. The camera zeros in for a close up of his face, pausing for a few seconds before it gradually pulls back to reveal Kid lying on a hospital bed.

He woke with the aura of his body still buzzing in horror, and the ceiling above him undulating like the waves of an ocean. His jaws ached. They had been locked for eighteen hours straight, grinding throughout the gruesome nightmares that he was now routinely plagued by. There was a metallic taste of blood in his mouth from his bleeding gums. Kid orbited his body like a satellite and caught the rank stench of an Astral dog steaming off him. He sighed heavily. He felt hollow, bereft, completely dead inside, like some crustacean creature that had had all it's guts ripped out, leaving just an empty shell.

Beams from the headlamps of passing cars swept across the ceiling as he listened to the noise of their engines fading into the distance. He zoned out for a while, daydreaming, mulling things over in his head. He gazed up at the artex ceiling, making out shapes and faces in the swirling patterns of paint. Images emerging like creatures breaking cover in the undergrowth. A white, gas-flamed sprite materialised with troll-like eyes and ice cream whipped hair billowing off its skull, followed by a sultry, Hispanic cowgirl striking a provocative, cheesecake pose. The dusky dreamboat reclines belly down, bare ass up, on a chaise lounge, her alluring features and curly, chestnut hair peeking out from under the brim of a white Stetson. The sexy siren looks down at him, a come-hither look in her eyes. She flashes a naughty, flirtatious smile then disappears into the artex abstraction. His eyes trace the outline of a seahorse, and then one of Dali's flying tigers jumps out at him...images momentarily brought to life, before fading back into obscurity. Other times he made out a monkey in the cockpit of a plane, its hand on the stick, and the flowing locks of the blonde beauty depicted on the book cover of Crowley's *Moonchild* novel. Even Lenin put in an appearance, pontificating on a podium in his long, dark overcoat.

Kid reached for the bottle of *Chlorpromazine Largactil* on the bedside table, unscrewed the lid, and popped two 25ml tablets into his mouth. He was suffering the flashbacks again. His head was fuzzy and whirring with nasty, vibrating sensations that made him feel like one of those aggravated deer scraping the irritating, velvet fuzz from their sensitised antlers down to the raw, pink, bloody bone. He felt ill at ease within his skin for months now, as if he had been blown out from the centre of his being, recoiling from behind his face, to a nebulous region, half in and half outside his body; like the way figures on a TV screen appear, surrounded by ghostly auras when there is bad aerial reception. Removed from the core, it was like trying to drive a car while stuck in the back of the trunk. He couldn't watch horror films anymore, and hadn't washed his hair in months, both brought on flashbacks. It was a grueling, harrowing existence. Lost in a schizophrenic twilight zone, haunting the outer margins of his mind.

In his drug diary Kid wrote: "Still heavily sedated I crash through the swing doors of the hospital ward and grab a cab home. We seem to travel back in time to the 1970s as we cruise the length of Arundel Street in Landport, for I see the scenery as it used to look back then. The deserted playground of Arundel Court School behind its high perimeter fence. The sweet shop next door with the *Walls* ice-cream advertising display on the pavement. The park where I roamed as a child, collecting caterpillars. The Viking pub on the corner of the next road that's now gone. I catch a fleeting glimpse of the veranda of Froxfield House beyond it. The cab slows to a crawl as we approach Canberra House, and as we pass the flat I will inhabit in twenty years time, I sneak a peek through the living room window to see who is living there now and how it was once furnished and decorated.

"Flash forward twenty years. Its night time and the menu from a computer screen is blown-up and projected onto the exterior of Melbourne House, an identical eight-story block of flats, standing at a right angle to Canberra House. Both structures were once-derelict Landport estates that have been rebuilt, redesigned and rechristened in response to the booming popularity of Australian daytime soaps.

"The word HEBEPHRENIA is selected from the menu and flashed up on screen, writ large on the facade of the building. I ride the elevator two floors up to my flat in Canberra House. The lift stops with a sudden jolt and the doors open onto the red carpeted vestibule. Spaced out, I whirl around disorientated and weightless, like a human balloon. Keeling over to one side, I hit the floor with a soft, gentle tap and bounce back up again, hot molten snot burning in my nose. Translucent tadpole sperms of light dart before my eyes, vanishing one by one as the dizzy spell wears off.

"I enter the screening room of the Goya Cinema in Tangier,

a stunningly elegant art deco film palace. Its interior decor of burgundy coloured walls and seating creates a cozy, womb-like ambience that never fails to make me feel sleepy. The film is just about to start. Tied to the back of the seats are weightless human heads that bob on the slight breeze from the air conditioning. The heads face towards the screen like a creepy audience, inane, fixed toothed grins painted on their frozen faces. The velvet curtains open onto a stage set lifted from an old MGM musical, displaying the cardboard scenery of a forest. As I venture through these artificial woods there is an almighty crash, the sound of a thousand doors slamming all at once. With the din still ringing in my ears, I swing around and find the forest floor littered with the strewn carcasses of hundreds of dead deer.

"I'm then buzzed through the entry doors of the newly designed tower block that's been built on the former grounds of Froxfield House. It's a cylindrical structure, hollowed out in the middle, with a courtyard garden boasting a cluster of tree ferns mounted in white marbled bases, the kind you often find in shopping malls.

"It's the middle of the night so the place is lit up, but it's only as I turn my eyes skywards that the sheer, staggering, magnitude of it all sinks in. It was like a modern day Tower of Babel, balcony floors stretching upwards for miles as far as the eye can see, tapering until they disappear into the stratosphere. This stunning, spectacular sight only marred by the washing lines that crisscross each other, draping laundry all the way up, and the clutter of television aerials and satellite dishes that reminds you that despite the size and architectural sweep, it's just another slum.

"Weirdly, although this city in the sky is quite obviously inhabited by millions of people, sound seems to have been swamped and smothered into a vacuum. This, I find out later, is due to the noise limiters that have been installed to muffle the cacophonous racket that would otherwise be generated by so many people living in a confined space on top of one another. The buildings' unique acoustics means you can just about make out the faint rumblings of households settling down somewhere in the distance. Every now and then you can hear the remote, querulous cries of a greeting child, strains of music, or semblances of far-flung chatter, but they are all processed, so that by the time these cascading sounds have travelled the immense distance to the ground they have largely petered out and arrive strained, diffused and muted."

Again the entity takes off like a rollercoaster, launching itself full pelt down the narrow, off kilter corridor of a haunted mansion. Twisting and turning along its way, it flies up two staircases, sweeping to the end of the upper landing before coming to an abrupt halt outside the door of the attic room.

FLASHBACK: Astral Boy is in the tunnel flicking through the copy of *CADAVERS*. He turns a page and his voice narrates as Professor Litvinov reads the transcript from his remote viewing. "I then came across newspaper photographs showing the human and canine remains found in the Somerstown district of my old home town, White City. The accompanying article reports how the strange arrangement of bones, found on a car bonnet, have been verified by the police as Chinese ideograms, and that the characters suggest the word "sacrifice." The article also quotes a health official who, having analysed the remains, claims to have discovered a deadly new viral strain in the DNA. Apparently, the authorities are looking into possible links between this and a spate of local deaths, in which the victims were all intravenous drug users. One line of enquiry put forward is that this viral strain may have been passed into the human chain by drug dealers cutting the ground, infected bones of Astral dogs into their "Chinese Rock" street heroin, for the hallucinogenic properties they contained. The health official warned of the extreme delusions and other psychotic side effects this lethal concoction could induce, and how prolonged usage was fatal."

***

It was like an exquisite watercolour come to life. A grey, Avalonian lake cloaked in a fine, wispy mist, wreathed by weeping willow trees. Beyond lay the drug rehab, a crumbling Victorian mansion nestled in the New Forest in the heart of the Hampshire countryside. It was Skyrise Kid's first night there and he had been assigned the attic room, communally known as "the fridge," due to its year-round sub-zero temperature. In fact, the room was so chill that whenever he exhaled the steam from his breath would billow out his mouth like cigarette smoke. It was Spartan...just a single bed beneath a white sloped ceiling, and a chipped, cream coloured dresser standing under a lattice window. It had that stale, musty old house smell he couldn't stand and retained a turn of the century feel that conjured the ghosts of a Victorian bygone era.

Suddenly the room dissolves as the bedroom reverts back to a long lost nursery. Two diaphanous figures appear, faint and flickering like the images of early cinema. Two young sisters with blonde, ringlet tresses play with their ornately crafted dolls house. To their right a riderless rocking horse nods back and forth. The wraiths evaporate like cloud vapours as the present room re-emerges.

A wuthering storm broke that evening, in what would become the first and only night of Kid's stay. He listened as the heavens seemed to collapse, ruptured by a thunder that cracked its whip and rumbled on like the sound of buildings being levelled by a wrecking ball on a demolition site. Kid shivered, fully clothed beneath the thin, insufficient blankets he'd been given, unable to stop his teeth from chattering, as he tried, unsuccessfully, to get off to sleep.

As he gazed listlessly out into the pitch blackness of the room, he suddenly saw a pinpoint of light opening before him. Within seconds it had inflated into a gaping vortex. Spiralling walls of red translucent tissue cells expanded and contracted, like a giant esophagus blown out from the insides. The portal, illuminated at its core by a green, conical laser beam of light that shone through infernal mists, produced a spectacular liquid sky.

Cramming to take it all in, Kid reeled back aghast as a giant, disembodied head zoomed out from within this inner sanctum, and whooshed right up to his face, flames trailing in its wake. Hovering in mid-air right in front of him, it looked like Satan, exactly like Satan. He was horned with those unmistakably yellow eyes, which though quite obviously bestial, imparted all too human looks and expressions. Strangely quizzical at first, as Satan's head cocked and tilted to one side, to study Kid's horror-struck face, then softening to marvel and delight at the enchanting effect his presence was having on his spooked subject. Ultimately, coming on all seductive as he bewitched Kid with his diabolic charisma, his hardening eyes fired up, ablaze with maleficent power. The rest of Satan's features seemed markedly more disfigured than were usually depicted. His pulped, mushy skin sloughed away in clumps, dripping like candle wax down his grotesquely putrefied puss.

As the swirling whirlpool of hell fanned behind him, anorexic, hollowed-eyed sylphs strayed out of the chasm. Inexorably wasting away, their nebulous bodies swam through the air, trailing tadpole tails. Rebel angels flaunted and paraded themselves, uncasing their battered wings. Their golden breast plates dulled and tarnished, where once upon a time they gleamed like varnish. Red, gargoyle faced demons with transparent embryo skin sauntered out, congregating with winged skulls and Bosch-like devils. Tormented souls whose twisted mouths wailed in eternal misery. The howling, guttural groans, like the eerie sound made when voices are slowed down on a tape recorder.

It was all too much for him now, and steeling himself, Kid squeezed his eyes shut, slung the covers off, and bolted out of bed. Lunging across the floor, he went smack into the wall and flicked on the light switch.

The next morning Kid did a bunk from the rehab. He decided to take a short cut through the forest to the train station to catch the early train back to White City. Before he split, the others told him that somewhere in the forest were the withered remains of a dead horse. Kid had laughed it off, but en route he came to an open clearing where he was startled to find three live horses suspended forty feet in the air above him, each of them coiled up in vines. Strung up between a ring of sturdy oaks, they were snared in a fiendish cat's cradle. The nags whinnied in discomfort, their emaciated frames slowly wasting away as the ever tightening vines cut into their already-bleeding flanks and muzzles.

A creaking sound, then a loud crack, diverted Kid's attention to an oak tree way ahead of him, and he watched as a dead horse clattered through the branches, it's dead weight crashing to the floor with a heavy boom and a rustle of leaves that reverberated throughout the forest. All the while languishing above him, the helpless horses swayed gently to and fro in their death hammocks.

Back in the screening room at the Psychic Research Center, white, ghostly trails of Unidentified Flying Objects are tracked on a wall-sized radar screen by two technicians in specs and lab coats. Professor Litvinov storms into the room, rushing towards the screen for a close-up look. The screen is coated in a heat resistant Pyrex film so that any evidence of "spirit traces" can be wiped clean away...

Flyaway mists buffet the immense, glacial ball of light as

136

it plummets through the stratosphere heading to earth. The crystal blue sphere contains a human skull, its mandible open ready to gnash. Ice water sloshes around inside it, like surf in a washing machine. Residents are out on the streets of White City, scanning the skies. They're frantic, sick with worry as they track the two white orbs descending from space. Spiralling to earth on a rotary trajectory, the spheres orbit one another on a wide arc, scouring the sky with sound. There is talk of black stars converging on the equator, and white gasses can be seen drawing off a crescent moon. Air raid sirens drone and fog horns bellow out from the ships in the harbour. Kid manages to make it home from the rehab just in time. As the balls of light come down, he sprints from the train station to Oldbury House. He scrambles under the kitchen table, where he finds Schizy, the family's snow-white cat in repose, as stately as a sphinx. The house begins to shudder as the strange orbs draw closer. It sounds like a tornado approaching. Even if they crash in another country far away, it is certain the shock waves from their impact will be seismic with cataclysmic consequences.

Kid clutches the cat to his chest and rushes out the back door. As he cocks his leg over the garden railings, Schitzy jumps out of his arms and runs over to the rose garden by Stratford House. There, she stalks the barbed bushes, preying on a colony of tiny, red eyed marsupials, who blind to the sunlight, are easy prey. As whirlybird seeds twirl down from the deciduous trees, she pounces on them, claws out, puncturing the napes of their necks with her teeth, to a mewling chorus of, high pitched squeals.

The evening sky turns crimson as *Red Eye Disease* descends over White City. Choking on the atmosphere, Kid sucks on a spray can of oxygen that he salvages from his back pack. His voice rasps in reaction to the toxic conditions, and in a split second he's vaporised, his incinerated body casting an ashy shadow, permanently engraved, on the bleached white concourse.

In his final diary entry Skyrise Kid wrote: "Whether you believe these accounts of alien abduction, or view them as symptomatic of something else, one thing that cannot be denied is that in most cases they have proven to be extremely traumatic ordeals for those who have experienced them. They have not been the uplifting experiences that films like *ET* or *Close Encounters* would have you believe, full of benevolent celestial beings trying to enlighten mankind and show earthlings the way. Such ideas just have no ring of truth to them. In the back of most people's minds, even so-called unbelievers, there's a comforting thought that once we die we do at least find some peace of mind after all the shit we've been through. So the shocking realisation that there is, in fact, no afterlife and the sole purpose of our existence here is to be studied and experimented on like lab rats is a truly terrifying prospect to envisage and behold."

The top floor of the Flatiron Building breaks its moorings and lifts off in to the sky, heading for outer space...

The aftermath. Years have passed since the strange orbs hit. Aerial footage of a ravaged White City, post impact. An eerily deserted wasteland of ruins and debris ridden streets. The blown-out shells of buildings, just roofless remnants of a skeletal city razed to rubble. The nave of the city's cathedral has crumbled, leaving just the high, arched window frame overlooking a gutted lectern. Rusted iron girders are all warped and bent back, sculpted into new shapes by hurricane winds. Looks like modern art. The levelled landscape has been plunged into an ominous, doom-laden darkness, the kind that foreshadows an imminent eclipse. Over in Somerstown the tower blocks are all struts and no guts, and the swing park has been left in rack and ruin. The swing frame itself has collapsed on one side, and just a broken seat dangles on a solitary chain. The monochrome grey sky looks like shattered glass, and the austere stillness conveys a hushed, desolate beauty.

From the other side, Astral Boy recalls his own demise: "As the black shutters of death slam down behind the eyes, there's a dislocating, physiological ache as death jettisons the soul. The spirit literally slips the skin. Rising up from the soles of the feet, it snags on ankle bones, sticks to rubbery, pink sinews, catches on knee caps and elbows and bony wrists, until it's released, leaving nerves twitching and flinching. The spirit, drawn up through the skull, cracks open the cranium.

"Once I move beyond the threshold of death to the other side I look back down and can't help but feel sorry for the empty shell I've left behind that once was my body. My spirit explodes in a fireball, flash burning the sky and stratosphere, sprinkling particles of stardust that shimmers like iridescent fish scales. Life leaves only a transitory mark, like my graffiti tags on the Jacob's Ladder footbridge in Landport, now painted over, so future generations will never know they, or I, ever existed.

"Running in sequence are the final three panels of a comic strip, each one showing a star speckled view of the cosmos. As I read across the series, each caption momentarily comes to life before dissolving right before my eyes, fading into blank, black nothingness."

www.ingramcontent.com/pod-product-compliance
Lightning Source LLC
Chambersburg PA
CBHW071957170626
46813CB00005B/1912

* 9 7 8 0 9 5 6 9 5 2 5 0 9 *